A 2140 545251 3

"Relentless is VERY REAL."　　　　　　　—98.7 KISS FM

"A pure winner from cover to cover."　　—Courtney Carreras,
　　　　　　　　　　　　　　　YRB magazine on *The Last Kingpin*

"Gripping."　　　　　　　　　　—*The New York Times* on *Push*

"Fascinating. Relentless has made the best out of a stretch
of unpleasant time and adversity…a commendable effort."
　　　　　　　　　　　　　　　—Wayne Gilman,
　　　　　　　　　　　　　　　WBLS News Director on *Push*

"Relentless redefines the art of storytelling　while seam-
lessly capturing the truth and hard-core real
desperation and struggle."

REL

08/10

　　　　Founder of the African American Liter

"Relentless is seriously getting his grind on."

"Relentless writes provocative stories that raise many questions but presents stories that everyone can relate to."
　　　　　　　　　　　　　　　—*Da Breakfuss Club*

"Relentless is on the forefront of a movement called street-
lit."　　　　　　　　　　　　　—*Hollywood Reporter*

"One of the leaders of a 'hip hop literature' revolution."
　　　　　　　　　　　　　　　—*Daily News*

"Self-publishing street lit phenomenon Aaron serves up a
smoldering batch of raw erotica and criminality."
　　　　　　　　　　　　　　　—*Publishers Weekly*

Russell Library
123 Broad Street
Middletown, CT 06457

ST. MARTIN'S PAPERBACKS TITLES
BY RELENTLESS AARON

Topless

Rappers 'R In Danger

Platinum Dolls

Seems Like You're Ready

Sugar Daddy

Triple Threat

To Live And Die In Harlem

The Last Kingpin

Push

BUMRUSH

RELENTLESS AARON

St. Martin's Paperbacks

NOTE: If you purchased this book without a cover you should be aware that this book is stolen property. It was reported as "unsold and destroyed" to the publisher, and neither the author nor the publisher has received any payment for this "stripped book."

This is a work of fiction. All of the characters, organizations, and events portrayed in this novel are either products of the author's imagination or are used fictitiously.

BUMRUSH

Copyright © 2006 by Relentless Aaron/Relentless Content.

Cover photograph © Jon Feingersh/Getty Images

All rights reserved.

For information address St. Martin's Press, 175 Fifth Avenue, New York, NY 10010.

ISBN: 978-0-312-94971-6

Printed in the United States of America

Relentless Content, Inc. trade paperback edition 2006
St. Martin's Paperbacks edition / July 2010

St. Martin's Paperbacks are published by St. Martin's Press, 175 Fifth Avenue, New York, NY 10010.

10 9 8 7 6 5 4 3 2 1

Thank you JULIE & FAMILY, TINY, TANISHA, CURT, AB, FRANK, DAWN, and of course, READERS THROUGHOUT THE WORLD for taking me all the way to the top with your FAITH, your COMMITMENT, and your ENCOURAGEMENT. Thanks also to TIFFANY WILLIAMS & STEVE STREETS for your support in Atlanta.

FOREWORD

Meet the leader of the crew. His name is Miles, and he's got a video camera positioned so that he is the subject. And pay close attention to the monitor so that you don't miss anything.

"Maybe this is too deep for TV, but I'm gonna say it anyway. When I look up into a dark sky, I can see stars. I know that I'm not imagining things. I know that what I see is real. The stars *do* exist, and bright as they are, it's likely that they're the suns of entire solar systems, such as the one that surrounds the Earth's sun. I've also done enough reading to know that any of those stars out there are so many million miles away, which says that my eyes and yours are like high-end telescopes, powerful enough to capture these images in our minds. So, to know that these devices are set within our faces, that these eyeballs of ours are the equivalent of two mobile cameras, and then to complete the picture with other such important tools, like the capability to talk, to move, to hear, to think and compute and recall, we'd have to be fools to ignore the overall gift of being human. Like most everyone else, we have the gift of being that thinking, feeling, walking, talking force of nature that can maneuver from point A to point B (from the dream conceived to the goal achieved) at will . . .

". . . And I got to wondering, that if this is all by design, why are certain things permitted while others are not? Why do we kill ourselves and others? And if that's not bad enough, why does nature kill us? Who or what really determines the rights and wrongs here? And in the end, who do we answer to for the decisions we make in life?

"And I bet now you're asking why I had to get all deep, when all you wanted to know about is my story of how me and a few of my buddies were diamond bandits. And my answer? I guess my mind is playing tricks on me again."

This is a story about decisions. Our decisions. We made them carefully, ruthlessly, unconsciously and eventually, desperately. This is a story about me and my buddies Gus Chambers, Elvis Evans and Sonny Stewart. It's about our risks . . . our individual focus on our very own stars in that dark sky called life.

CHAPTER ONE

Against the dark sky the rain fell so hard it looked like knitting needles were shooting down in the night. A good thing, Miles was thinking, figuring that the robbery would go down so much easier this way. He was sure that the heavy rain would create a constant diversion, just because these particular black folks that the four had intended on robbing appeared to be afraid of getting wet. Maybe more afraid, Miles hoped, than they were careful to protect themselves.

"Yo, this is gonna be a cinch," Gus proclaimed from the back seat of the Mercedes. And even Gus's mind was preoccupied since the luxury car they sat in belonged to neither him, Miles or Sonny. In fact, this car was a top-of-the-line Mercedes that belonged to Sonny's mom, thanks to the hard work she put in at General Foods. She had that no-risk lifestyle and those traditional disciplines that made owning a Mercedes Benz possible, which is exactly why Sonny had to wait until his moms fell asleep to sneak off with it. He figured he'd only be a couple of hours; three hours at most. And he definitely had to be back in time enough so that his pop would see it in the driveway when he got in from 3rd shift at the bus company.

Sonny checked his Ironman watch for the umpteenth time and said,

"Why don't we just take 'em now. Just run up on the fool, snatch his shit and be out."

"Cool it, Sonny. You know we can't just hit this dude all up in front of the club. Even in the rain people would make us. Whassup wit'chu?"

Sonny seemed to come down from the hype and tension and said, "I just wanna get this shit over with." Again checking the watch.

"Lemme' find out you gotta get home 'fore your curfew," said Gus with the lazy eye and scar just underneath it. His face looked normal for the moment all scrunched up in his hearty laugh.

"Listen, dark child," Gus retorted. But then Sonny appeared to have every intention of snapping; Gus again with the cracks about Sonny's oh-so-dark complexion, something his peers teased him about all his life.

". . . least I got a family. Don't make me keep it real wit' you. I'll hurt yo' feelings quick." Sonny heard himself sink into the slang, felt himself pulled to the defensive side; the fight that surfaced when his ego was challenged. So what if he had that good upbringing. That didn't stop him from blending in or conforming to the ways of the street.

"Y'all need to stop. Dude's on his way out," said Miles.

The three were casing Matchstick, just as they had every Friday night for the past 3 weeks. It was Sonny who spotted the baller, identifying him as a "bling-bling man." With the rocks on Matchstick's two pinkies, the three or four chains n' whatnot dangling from his right earlobe, Sonny figured the man to have at least thirty grand in jewels. The watch alone had to be enough for a down payment on a house. Furthermore, Matchstick had these two fly cuties on his arms, the full-length fox fur coat, the pimp hat to match. Then, of course, he was flashin' that wad of cash at the bar inside the club, as well as he had the newest Jag a man could drive parked outside. Just like he did last Friday night, Matchstick strolled into Manhattan Proper on Linden, then into Gordon's on Hillside, and then from

Queens, he crossed over into midtown Manhattan where he glided into the Shadow, known to all as New York's Longest Running Adult Nightclub. But it was close to twelve now and the three decided the waiting was over; no more following this cat around town. It was time to make the move.

The sign in the parking lot was clear. Obviously there was the word **PARK** in bright red letters, and smaller letters that quoted the $5.75 per hour charge. But the even smaller print told the real story: "Not responsible for property after midnight." Essentially, if you were patient and savvy enough to read between the lines, the inference here was that there was no attendant to watch the vehicles after twelve. Nonetheless, this was the only parking lot within a block of the Shadow. Any other parking was strictly go-for-self along the curbs of 28th street, just another part of the city that hookers, homeless and ne'er-do-wells called home. By day this area was ridden with the traffic of delivery trucks, taxis and other commercial vehicles trying to cross-town or take short cuts to avoid the bumper hugging that often congested 10th, 8th and even Avenue of the Americas. By night the block was lit up with sports cars, SUV's and luxury cars, all with their glossy black tires, chromed-out rims and glistening waxed exteriors. These were the players and the hustlers of the underground who where comfortable with the night and the surroundings that bespoke of their own life's mysteries and dark sides. These were the white collar and blue collar workers who suited up and showed-out in effort to keep up with the ballers; some of them unable to afford the lifestyle they projected, yet happy to pretend; happy just to be a part of the mix. These were the ladies that buddied up into duos, threesomes and so forth, combining their resources to add some spice to their lives even if it would fade and eventually dissipate like their expensive perfumes, glossed lips and diva hairstyles, all in the effort to put their best foot forward. Maybe they'd impress an NBA star or an accomplished producer. Maybe they'd run into Maxwell, Malik or Michael. Maybe.

The chick on the left of Matchstick held an umbrella big enough for the both of them. The chick on the right, walking body-to-body aside of Matchstick, held an umbrella all to herself. Both of his chicks had on mini skirts, high heels, fishnet stockings and halter tops for their midsections to show. Both of them had the long weaves and jewelry that served more as labels than accessories. *Didn't they watch the weather reports?* And now the three of them strutted (slow enough to seem cool, but fast enough to wanna stay dry) out from under the Shadow's canopy and along the sidewalk towards the parking lot. All the while their backs were turned, unaware of the threat coming towards them.

The lot still had a couple dozen vehicles parked, their bold owners still getting that dance on in the club. And the vehicles were positioned so that the three had to break ranks to pass through the narrow spaces in between. A sudden vigorous thumping disturbed the atmosphere, but neither Matchstick or his chicks acknowledged the sounds for what they were. It sounded too much like thunder, but indeed it was the half dozen footfalls rushing up from behind, making their impact on the hoods and trunks of various parked vehicles. Like trappers after the living, or vultures preying on the dead, Miles, Gus, and Sonny made their abrupt, noisy climb, ready to swoop down and overcome Matchstick and company.

"Slow ya' roll," chopped Gus, who had the huskiest voice out of the three.

Then Sonny said, "Yo' playa, it's ya birthday."

All three assailants were 20-something, with their wooden bats raised, waiting for the slightest threat. Meantime, Miles paid specific attention to Matchstick, wondering if he'd cower or if he's play hero in front of the women. All 6ft and 195 pounds of Gus hopped down from a car's hood, almost bouncing off like the pouring rain, and he pushed Matchstick against an adjacent car.

"Da' fuck y'all want from me? You know who the fuck I am?"

"Yeah," Gus said with no dissension at all. "You's the next niggah."

"What?" replied Matchstick, the rain soaking into his hat and fox fur, matting them both down till they appeared oil-slicked. And you could see his loafers were less than comfortable, soaked like he'd gone swimming in them.

"I said you's the next niggah . . . the next niggah to get took. Now get y'hands up on the car!"

Everything was moving fast now. While Gus pressed the business-end of the bat

up against the hustler's spine, Sonny and Miles attended to the women.

"That's alright, baby. You can keep the umbrella up to keep that ass dry. Just turn around and I'll help you get out the necklace." And while Miles reached for the necklace, the bracelet, then the earrings, Sonny was doing the same with the other woman, only in his own way. No, she couldn't hold up her umbrella; it was already on the ground collecting rain. He had her with her arms, not her hands, up on the hood of a car. Meanwhile he pressed the handle of the bat against her lower back, the rain doing major damage to her 75-dollar-hairdo and streaming down her neck, along her shoulders and down the sinewy build of her back. Sonny licked the drops from his upper lip as he indulged in a horny man's look at the baller's babe. Why couldn't he work with anything this fine, Sonny wondered, however briefly. All he had to work with was Dori from back around the way. Dori, the aspiring singer. After a quick peek to see what the other two were doing – and they were certainly handling their end of the job – Sonny wiped most of the wetness from his brow and down to his chin. Then he eased up on the cocoa cutie and used one hand to unfasten the chain around her neck. With the bat in his other hand, he reached around and under her raised arm to pull the handle of the bat and his inner wrist up against her cleavage. He was that close to her . . . close enough for the both of them to share the same rain drops. Close enough to smell her. After all, he was in charge. The woman was shaken but she managed to utter a defense.

"You ain't gonna rape me too, are you?"

"Sonny!" Miles called out. "Stick to business, man – shit."

Miles had most of his victim's valuables already. Sonny sucked his teeth, and realizing he was having a tough time getting the chain loose, he made a frustrated tug at it.

"Ouch," the woman cried when it jerked off of her neck.

"Shun'ta opened your mouth. It could'a been nice," Sonny said, still disappointed that he couldn't get his groove on. Then he turned and saw Gus going through the man's wallet.

"Gus!"

Sonny's shouting alerted Miles who was the closest. Miles immediately lifted his bat and swung it at Match-stick who had reached for and got a grip on the pistol at his waist.

"Shit!" Sonny said. And now Miles struck again, this time at Matchstick's arm. And now Sonny swung as well, only he went for the baller's head. There were two shouts, one of them from the first hit, and another exasperated grunt following the second. Matchstick was falling to the pavement, his pistol before him.

"Whoa, whoa, whoa," snapped Miles, reaching to prevent Sonny from a fourth swing.

"Don't kill the muh'fucka, Son. Damn."

"Let's be out," said Gus. "We got what we came for."

They started off.

"Hold up," said Gus. "I didn't get the watch."

In the meantime Sonny was in the cute one's ear again. "When he wakes up . . . tell 'em the boys from Jersey said happy birthday." Then Sonny smacked the woman's wet ass and bounced.

At the edge of the lot, all three shed their green nylon

aviator jumpsuits. Miles balled them up and stuffed them, the jewels, and what he could of the weapons into a tennis bag. The Mercedes was still double-parked across the street from the lot. But, even the short trot back to the car left them drenched with rain.

"Shake it off," Sonny told his conspirators before they got in the car. His mother would kill him.

CHAPTER TWO

"No food until afternoon," Miles had told the others. "This way we'll be hungry, alert. Just like they do boxers before a big fight." But that was more than 12 hours ago. Now, the so-called fight was over. They won. It was time to eat.

"Shit man, I don't wanna get in no damn argument over where to grub out. Just stop at M and G's on the way back uptown," Miles said.

Gus wanted to stop at the McDonald's drive thru and Sonny said he wanted to get home . . . said he was uptight and stressed out.

"Why can't y'all just eat at home? Bad enough we hot right now." Sonny was saying this as the Mercedes made the trip up the West Side Highway about to hit the 125th street exit.

"It ain't that bad, dog. A ma-fucka prob-ly still layin' in the rain waitin' on EMS. Blood all in his fur."

"Man, you were close to gettin' your cabbage twisted, Gus," mentioned Miles.

"If it wasn't for Sonny all up on that hooker, I'da been focused."

"You s'pose ta' be focused anyway," snapped Sonny.

Gus sucked his teeth and said, "Whatever, just lemme' get some Micky-Dees."

"How bout this," Miles said, wanting to break up a conversation that was getting nowhere. "We do the quick drive-thru, I pick up a quickie at M and G's, and we all go home and eat there."

"Fine by me. As long as y'all don't eat in the car. I ain't tryin' to clean up no more than I have to."

Gus rolled his eyes wondering why they couldn't come up with that conclusion in the first place.

While they waited in line behind 4 other cars, Miles said, "That was too close. Too damned *close*." And he squeezed his fists together, gritting his teeth as he spoke. "We said that we were supposed to be safe *at all times. No risk.* That was the deal."

"It ain't like it wasn't possible, Miles. Anything is always possible."

"But, dude had a gun. We ain't *never* run into *that*. I mean, okay, if he *had* a gun is one thing, but he actually had it *in his hand. He could'a got a shot off* at any one of us."

Sonny was back to looking at his watch. Then he said, "Well maybe we gotta change the game."

"Say what?"

"Change the game. We can't go to a knife fight with fists, and we can't go to a gun fight with knives."

Miles sucked his teeth knowing that the suggestion was both very right and very wrong.

He said, "And if we gotta do somebody?"

"Hey Miles," Sonny said. "*You* the one bitchin' about *dude had a gun.* If I had a gun tonight, and I saw what I saw? *Ain't no question* what I woulda done."

"Yeah, okay Mister Murder. I'm just sayin' there's a bigger price to pay if we do the gun move. The robberies we been doin' with no guns wouldn't get us no time if we got caught. But a gun? An armed robbery? *Psssh.*"

"But you said the right shit, son. *If* we get caught. How the fuck we gonna get caught? We done four of these now. Got this shit down to a science. This ain't like a bank job or a Brinks job, dog. This is John-Q-public we gettin' at. Sweet as cherry pie."

"So then you're down with this too, Gus? I mean, you wanna change the game? Step it up?"

"I'm down for whatever. Semper Fi, dog."

Semper Fi. "*Always faithful*." The term followed Miles like a nightmare. And when the phrase came up now and then there was no choice but to recall the stint he did in the United States Marine Corps. The trials and tribulations . . . the troubles he experienced as a recruit on Parris Island, South Carolina. Marine Corps Boot Camp.

The recruiter at the Fordham Road Station told Miles this might happen, that the drill instructors might treat him differently because he was a street smart kid from the Bronx. Never mind that he just might be naturally more alert or sharp or a fast thinker with that built-in sixth sense, the gestures and mannerisms to go with it. Just the words "Bronx" or "New York" denoted a sense that, sight unseen, Miles was likely a trouble maker amongst the 80 recruits in his platoon. But it was too late to double-think now. Miles was signed-up, sworn-in and swept-up into a world that had its own rules; they called it regimented. Essentially, this is the way it was, the way it is, and the way it was gonna be. Parris Island was suddenly the beginning of a dream come true, or else a prison of the worse kind; a prison of the mind.

This experience was designed, they said, to break down and then to build up a "real" man. A machine designed to act and to take orders without fear. Regardless of a man's origin, his size, or whatever he'd been through up until age 18, this 90-day, 3-stage program was said to handle the task of that all-important evolution. These training exercises would first shock Miles until he'd piss his camouflage cargo pants, they'd degrade and humiliate him so that he'd "unlearn" whatever bad habits or routines he knew from back home, and then they'd brainwash him with the world of "the few, the proud."

* * *

They shocked Miles by constantly shouting in his ear, imposing their authority over him by ordering him to do what they wanted, when, and how fast. And this was merely during the first two weeks when new recruits were housed in a wood frame building, issued a duffel bag full of necessities, clothed, shaved to the scalp, expected to study some basic training Marine Corps rules and norms, and counted a number of times throughout the days and nights to be sure that no one was frightened to the point of suicide or worse, trying to escape from Parris Island and facing those fabled alligators lurking in the surrounding swamps. It wasn't hard to control the recruits if you controlled the man's basic needs. Food. Sleep. The ability to think. Contact with loved ones back home. These could sound novel to the citizen outside of the military. But on the inside, the impact no less than controlled a man's ability to breathe.

By his third week on Parris Island, Miles was finally assigned to platoon 3002, part of the 3rd Battalion. He was among dozens of others who took that early morning stroll along asphalt roads and a wooded path to reach the red brick building, one of many 3-level structures known as squad bays. It seemed as if the woods they'd trekked through were an equivalent to a passage; one that had been traveled by hundreds of others. Finally, the new recruits had left behind those monotonous weeks of orientation, a welcoming that was not the warmest or coziest, but at least (as far as Miles was concerned), it was something that was bearable. After all, didn't every candidate watch those boot camp videos over and over again at the recruiting station? Wasn't this to be expected?

Not necessarily. On the receiving end of that passage the soft Corps (if that's what one assumed it to be) began to dissipate and the hard Corps (the "hard-core" realities) began to set in. It was as if they'd stepped into a living Hell, one that videos or that word of mouth could've never prepared them for. The yelling and shouting seemed to escalate to decibels familiar only to roller coaster fanatics. The imminent threat and unyielding authority of the three Marine Corps drill instructors brought a sense of tension and pressure that was something like deep sea diving, where all you could do was go with the flow, no matter how much or how little breath you had. You were NOT in control. The world (like the force of the merciless sea) closed in around their bodies. Little or no opportunity to breathe. And they wouldn't let down, ordering all 80 recruits to strip down to nothing where in most cases they'd never stood naked before or beside another man. This humiliation, to have a perfect stranger— ewww! *A* man!—inspect their bodies was just the start. Even if it did balance the playing field amongst the blacks, the whites and the others, it was most humiliating. And the recruits stripped so often that it became normal; part of being that "green machine" the Corps was accustomed to building. You were no longer Black or White or of Asian or Latino descent. No. "Now you belong to me! Now you're green!"

Any gripes expressed whether by expression or inaction were subject to severe punishment. Push ups. Deep knee bends. Running in place. All of the above, until the beads of sweat reached your toes. Punishment like you never felt. Until you passed out and some of that cold, ugly water splashed your face. And even then, you'd be back to the squad bay, in front of the devil-eyed drill instructor for more of the same. Suddenly, the dream of being one of the "few and the proud" was a trap.

Just days after the recruits were assigned to their platoons and to the drill instructors who would dominate their lives for 3 months, M-16 rifles were issued. Suddenly, this experience wasn't sleep-away camp, a grown-up's boy-scout camp or military school. It wasn't just scary anymore. For Miles to have this rifle in his possession was suddenly fateful. And all *80 recruits* had weapons; a firearm that they had to sleep with and be responsible for. A weapon that gave them the wherewithal to kill.

If things hadn't already turned serious in the preceding 3 weeks, this new climb up and into that 90-day training left Miles with the eerie confusion of importance and doom. This is my rifle. This is my gun. This is for work. This is for fun.

CHAPTER THREE

In the underworld of New York City, whether you committed crime, or if you were simply demonic by how you survived or with whom you associated, you had to at least hear about Rose. He was a thug who many said was the spitting image of Tupac, the hip hop icon. Except Rose was older now. And, of course, Rose was still very much alive. No, he didn't rap, and he didn't have an urge to. As the foremost underground gun dealer in the region, he couldn't afford any publicity, good or bad. And besides, his roots were already thick with tragedy of a father committed to life in the penitentiary, and pregnant with a Brooklyn-bred background; street hustles, gang wars, violence and loss of life. It was natural for Rose to blend in with the lawlessness of life with his tight body, the heart of a dynamo, and on top of all that readiness where he survived and took on challenges. He dealt guns. That's all anyone knew about him. Of course there were the street stories, rumors really, of how he was somehow behind the shooting . . . the one up in Co-Op City a few years back when a young woman named Toya shot the notorious Freeze at point-blank range. It was an execution that put a stop to the thousand kilo-plus per month cocaine dynasty that Freeze operated. And after all, Toya was a cousin to Rose. So, anything was possible. Needless to say, folks feared Rose. He was one of the few who "qualified" as fearsome, no smoke and mirrors and slick talk to create the illusion of a thug. And if you thought twice about it, Rose couldn't even be called a thug anymore, since that would underestimate him.

Elvis Evans was waiting for Rose when he met Melanie at the Jimmy's Bronx Café. He could've choked on his own saliva, she was so fine. She had a face like Beyonce, a body bangin' like Jennifer Lopez, and that sassy, feisty attitude like Rosie Perez. She was the best of all those worlds and then some. Elvis found himself all caught up in her jet black hair, how it was pulled back to the crown of her head and then left in wet, bushy, flowing tendrils beyond that.

"Can I get you somethin'?" She asked, her Latin apparent and blending nicely with that tangy Bronx flavor.

"Just a rum and Coke," Elvis replied, and then he looked down at his watch, not wanting to be too obvious about his instant crush on Melanie's stunning features. Somewhere in the back of his mind, behind the infatuation, the lust and the want to penetrate and be penetrated by this woman, underneath all of all that, Elvis knew he'd never be so lucky. Someone this beautiful in such a high profile spot; *a bartender? At Jimmy's? Surely*, she had to be taken. Surely some Latin king* like Fat Joe, or Ricky Martin or the Golden Boy, or any of the legions of wannabees that looked up to them . . . surely somebody had stepped to her already. Made her his own.

"You new around here?" Melanie asked him.

He had to think about that one. Ever since Parris Island he felt as though he'd come to rejoin the human race from some planet beyond the moon.

"You could say that. You really could say that," Elvis replied, his head clouded with all of those memories, all of them racing through his mind and then leaving him demented like a crash test dummy.

"I just got out of boot camp. Marine Corps."

---

*Note: This term is used as an endearing title, not a gang affiliation.

"Oh yeah? No kiddin'. How was that?"

The question was both painful and therapeutic. He needed to share all of these harbored emotions with somebody, or else he'd go nuts. However his answer was half-a-lie. Parris Island was more than 6 months behind him. And he'd uttered the words intending to earn her sympathies, which was working.

Elvis turned his head, casually panning the café to see if his appointment had arrived. He figured there was time to at least impress his new friend. Or try to.

"It wasn't easy," he said, deflating some air through his lips and wagging his head. "You go down there expecting one thing and they give you something totally different. In other words, they beat the shit out of you." Elvis was trying his best to appear depressed, but not so much as to not behold that glimmer of hope. If only someone could help him over that hump . . .

"But now it's over," said Melanie. "You're a Marine now. I'd say it paid off. Somethin' for your baby to be proud of."

Elvis was reminded now that he did feel like an accomplished Marine. He still had his high-n-tight buzz cut, the tough jawed expression and the rock hard body. Certain things you couldn't get away from.

"Sure. I guess you're right. You think I can still measure up out here? All these ballers with their fancy rides and flashy jewels? You think I'm still worthy of a nice . . . companion?"

"Psssh. Oh please! These floozies? Half of 'em still live with their mothers, and the other half, the ones who know how to keep a job, they bore me."

"So you sayin' you don't appreciate a hard workin' man?" Elvis leaned more into the conversation.

Melanie leaned in as well, then she responded, "Oh I definitely appreciate that, a hard worker and all. But I don't want no okie-dokie on my arm. I'm *today's* women. Today's woman is interested in a man who's an achiever. Today's man is the one who's made somethin' incredible out of very little means. He's got ingenuity and goals and some goddamned destiny ahead of 'em."

Elvis was feeling a bit burdened all of a sudden, as though he was getting more than he asked for. Why was she speaking to him as if he were her brother? Didn't she see him as a potential suitor? Was it the military reference? Did she, maybe, empathize with soldiers as a result of recent news events?

"So then a Marine isn't today's man?" Elvis asked the question intending to challenge the bartender, feeling perhaps that he had been right all along, that she wasn't likely to want someone like him.

Melanie had both arms on the bar and she was leaning in just enough for cleavage to show under her burgundy silk spandex tube dress.

"I don't know," she said, her eyes doing that sensual toe-to-head bit.

"I guess it depends on, uhm . . . which Marine we're talkin' about?" Elvis and Melanie's eyes were glued to one another. At that instant there were ideas and experiences and promises shared with no need for words.

"Excuse me," a woman's voice interrupted. "Are you Elvis?"

"Uh . . . yeah," he replied, finding it hard to pull away from the sudden magnetism. "Who's askin'?"

Now Elvis realized what the young woman wanted as she hinted to a table set by a far wall.

"Oh." And Elvis turned to say something in parting but the bartender had glided off to tend to another customer.

That was him, thought Elvis. Sure as the night giving way to day, that was him. Rose didn't appear to be any different than Elvis remembered, just more at ease. As if he was in his essence, protected by intrigue and wrath combined; characteristics which were very welcome in New York City. And wasn't he also wearing red when they first met on the Greyhound coming to New York from the Carolinas?. The red baseball cap with the "R" embroidered in white. The red flight jacket and blue jeans. The diamond cross draped around his neck, like the rappers do. And it wasn't one, but two women with him. Not with him as women in love are with men, but with him, like some kind of personal security. Neither the one leading Elvis, nor the one posted by Rose at the table was dressed in skirt and high heels. No. These could've been biker chicks, if Elvis knew no better. Except, weren't they too pretty to be biker chicks? Weren't they too disciplined in their expressions to be mere tag-a-longs who piggybacked on Harleys and lived to exhibit their breasts or their newest tattoos?

"Sup," said Rose.

Elvis gave the feared gangster a nod. As he shook hands he told himself that he had to get accustomed to these handshakes, the kind that was common in the hood. Elvis had been so into the businessman's face and gestures; so into pretending just so that he might be accepted for this job or that. Trying to blend back in with mainstream civilian life, so much so that he'd nearly laid to rest his South Bronx customs.

"Yo'," answered Elvis as he yielded to the woman's appraising eyes. In another world Elvis would be pushing up on the woman, asking for a date or a dance.

"With the bodyguards you got I wouldn't wanna be your enemy."

"Without them you wouldn't wanna be my enemy," Rose affirmed after putting down his drink. Then he said "You look like you put on a few pounds since we took that ride from down the way."

"Just getting relaxed, gettin' into the swing of things, I guess."

"You think you ready to get down wit' us?"

"I'm hungry, man. I'm ready fo' sho'."

"I know you said you handled that M-sixteen and all, but how much you really know about munitions? If I showed you a dozen firearms could you name 'em?" Rose examined Elvis carefully not just wanting to hear a response, but also watching for his expression. The eyes never lied even if the lips or the heart did.

"I can't lie to you, man. All I know is a few automatic weapons. I know the nine millimeter, I know the Glock, of course I know the M-Sixteen and M-One rifles . . . took them apart and put 'em together with my eyes closed while I was down in training. We handled grenades, too."

"What about shotguns? You ever touch pump actions? Twelve gauges or sawed-offs?"

Elvis wagged his head. Then he said, "But I'm a fast learner."

"Most of what we're pushin', especially in the hood, is nines and Rugers. Stuff that's small enough to conceal . . ."

Rose explained this but the bottom line to him was not so much whether or not Elvis had extensive knowledge. What meant most was his loyalty and trust. Rose caught on to that within the first hour on that bus trip. Sure, it was over 6 months back, but he'd never forget what he took from their conversation. Elvis had grown a strong hate for the government. He'd lost all respect for authority. Rose figured out some of the story, especially the things Elvis was put through down in Parris Island. Except it seemed that there was so much more piled up in Elvis. Things he didn't reveal. Rose offered the discharged man some words of wisdom, told him that a new life was waiting for him. But those words seemed to travel in one ear and right out the other. There were some other issues there. Still, Rose saw that Elvis had a desire . . . that he still had that desire to serve honorably, to be faithful and dutiful. It was just that he'd have nowhere to commit that energy. That's when Rose told himself that he'd help this guy. He'd give him a start.

Elvis took a while to agree with the human race again. There was no sensitivity training to help him through this, through this merge back into society. So instead of things being fresh and new, they were small, awkward or appalling. Instead of brilliance, he recognized gloom in that tough climb ahead of him. Job after job accepted him for his discipline, his work ethics and surely his false testimony about being Honorably Discharged. Maybe they took him in for his good looks. But once he got a grip of what really occurred, that slave-master relationship and the do-as-you're-told superiority over him, Elvis immediately pulled out. It was one job after another. Fast food franchises, department store positions, restaurant jobs and the caddie hustle at the local golf course. There was always an abundance of jobs waiting, and he was always more than qualified. But Elvis had this cancer inside of him that not even he could explain. And since he couldn't explain it, he certainly couldn't do anything about it.

Now that he ran into Rose, there was something he could finally be proud about. In a wicked sort of way, this anti-government independence of dealing guns to the thugs from around the way filled Elvis with a sense of contribution. Rose said that it was simple. Cut and dry. Set up the sale, determine what weapons were wanted, needed or required, then make the delivery. Elvis would be a middle man, at least. At most, he'd be an independent contractor. A weapons specialist. This was bigger than the military. This was exciting and adventurous, to deal with hoodlums and crooks on a business level. They'd need him. They'd respect him. As long as he didn't cross over into Rose's territories, he'd be fine. Stay out of Brooklyn, first and foremost, Rose had explained. And you might as well stay away from the Italians, too. Rose's roots ran deep and there was no sense in stepping on his toes. Like they said, don't cut off the hand that feeds you.

Elvis figured he'd stick to the magic of the BX. It was such a widespread web of connections; the Latin Kings, the gangs on the east side, the murder-crews up in Soundview, the Gun Hill Crew. Maybe he'd try further north, to Mt. Vernon and Yonkers, if he got the chance.

CHAPTER FOUR

"I promise you I'll get it back before four, Ma. I just need to make a quick trip downtown," Miles pleaded.

"Mmm hmm, that's what you said the other day. But I ended up callin' in late for work. And I can't afford to lose pay. I'm already takin' care o' you and payin' . . ."

"Ma, listen. If you let me go now, I'll not only get the car back by three thirty, but I'll also have three hundred for you."

"Miles Green, you got more lies than a king size bed. Where you gonna get three hundred, much less thirty dollars? You ain't even got no job."

"But I got my lil' hustles, Ma. Just trust me, okay? Just this once. I might surprise you and come home with a brand new car."

"Mmm hmm, and my name is Aunt Jemima."

"Three hundred three thirty," Miles nearly sang the reminder.

"Well, alright. But if I have to call in to work—"

"You won't, Ma." Miles stepped up and kissed her real quick and snatched the keys from the kitchen counter before saying, "Love you."

"Mmm hmm, love you, too."

Miles was ecstatic. It was only 12 noon. Time enough to pick up Bambi, (his girlfriend, the aspiring singer), shoot into the city, cash in the jewels, and then take Bambi to a fly restaurant. Maybe he'd even have time to buy her a little

something from one of those snazzy shops along 5th avenue.
From his mother's apartment on Warburton Avenue, the north-
end of Yonkers, Miles took the late model Pontiac, gliding
like a blue jay on a calm wind across town to Rumsey Road.
Bambi was there at her pop's house for the week. That was
her situation; 7 weeks with her mom in Newark, New Jersey
and 1 week with her father in Yonkers. It had been that way
for as long as Miles knew her; ever since he ran into her at
the Yonkers Mall. She was shopping with a friend. (She was
always shopping with a friend.) And Miles searched the
depths of his courage cabinet to step to her with his best approach; his "A Game." He was just weeks out of boot camp
at the time, looking fit and tanned. Any woman would've
wanted him.

Bambi had been sassy that instant, questioning the nerve
that Miles had to pop up and interfere with her shopping.
She looked him up and down and cocked her head when he
approached, wondering to herself, what could he do for me?
Then he flashed a smile that broke her right in half. She took
her hand off of her hip and came up out of that hooker's
pose. He babbled something about her being "very beautiful" and "sweet on his eyes," but in the world according to
Bambi, what else was new? In the end he romanced a phone
number out of her (the New Jersey number) and he used it
sparingly. A little strategy came into play, where Miles gave
his new friend her space, but in the meantime he injected
more and more of who he was into her consciousness. Even
if Miles was fishing for (and catching) his fair share of round-
the-way girls who pleasured him, Bambi was heavy on his
mind. It helped that she was out of reach too, either in New
Jersey or with her father. This way there was some anticipation. Unlike the girls he saw from day to day, Bambi left
something to the imagination. When she finally agreed to
date Miles, he took her to a Wesley Snipes flick, to Mr.
Smorgasbord, and then straight home.

So much anticipation built up during the date that the
long-awaited good night kiss sent shivers up Bambi's spine.

And it was clear that Miles felt the urge to press on, but then he pulled back, apparently in an effort to show respect. Yet, his Mister Nice Guy ways only made Bambi want for more; had her sitting near the phone for days waiting for his next call.

While Bambi waited, Miles (at the time) had been planning and then executing his crew's 2nd lick, the move they made on a drug dealer up in Bridgeport Connecticut. The 3 trips they took up interstate 95, coupled with the time it took to trace the dealer's footsteps and get a fix on his routine, turned out to be worth the effort. Eventually, the three overpowered him as he made a pick up. When they were done pillaging his pockets, they locked him in the trunk of his BMW and headed back to New York with seven grand in cash, the dealer's Rolex watch and a diamond encrusted medallion that was molded into a king's crown. After cashing in the diamonds, the three split up the money into $7,000 each.

With his money, Miles paid off an overdue college loan, he paid for new tires and brakes for his mom's Pontiac and with the remaining $3,000 he and Bambi did the town. This was their 2nd date, and it happened to fall on Bambi's 19th birthday. Eventually, things got so involved that they stretched the celebration into a whole weekend. Bambi had her friend cover in case her father called to check up, and she left with Miles on a trip to Disney World and Sea World down in Florida. They took Delta, they rented a car, and they shacked up in a hotel on the outskirts of the theme park, in Orlando. It was during that weekend that Bambi finally . . . finally gave Miles admission into her own amusement ride. The loving went on for a long thirty minutes. It ended abruptly when hotel security charged into their room unannounced; or it seemed unannounced. But this wasn't the police raid that Miles thought it to be; they panicked in response to Bambi's screams and cries. The hotel security had knocked and knocked, but the knocking went unheard, drowned out by her joyful noise.

Bambi was glued to Miles all the way back home. She even got into an argument with her father over her lying about where she'd gone. The suntan gave her away. So to help her ease the tension, Miles FedExed her a $1,500 gold necklace.

On their next date he bought her a fur coat and an elegant evening gown, vowing to soon take her out to an event where she'd have to wear it. And again they made love until the cops came knocking at their motel door.

Now that the three succeeded with their 4th lick, and that Miles was about to realize another nice chunk of change, he intended on getting a little more serious with Bambi. It wasn't just that she was absolutely drop dead gorgeous, or that she had the potential to be an accomplished singer. It didn't even have much to do with how outrageous the lovemaking was . . . not as much, anyway. What inspired Miles most about this young woman, all five-five of her, with bedroom-brown eyes and a vicious body, was that she had the most love for him that he'd ever experienced from a woman. It was a love that promised so much more, but always left him wanting. It was energy that left him both satisfied, but strung out. As if Bambi was an ocean of pleasure that brushed up on his shores, teasing him to come and jump in all the way. For all he knew, this was love. All the love he'd ever need.

"Did you get the down payment for your truck yet?" Bambi asked this not a moment after she got in the Pontiac, maybe tired of the whole mother-son bit. Maybe helping to push Miles towards his own independence.

"Not yet. I should have most of it today, after the trip to the city." Miles was still relieved that his Moms lent him the ride till 3:30.

"Oooh! The city?' A gigantic smile opened across Bambi's face. The city always meant either auditions or shopping. And no. she didn't have an audition scheduled for today.

"Yeah, but . . ." Miles had to stop himself, not wanting to

reveal how short a trip it would be, but ever aware of the time just the same. He found himself trying to satisfy both his mother and his girlfriend.

"Well, let's just say there's a surprise in store."

Bambi with the glistening teeth under those glossed lips.

"It's been a minute ya' know," she said reaching over into Miles lap. But he saw the gesture as less than genuine—as though she wanted to show gratitude for a forthcoming gift. This was a first. It also depressed Miles at a time that should have been spontaneous as he could stand. Was this why Bambi was glowing? Because of his next gift? Or maybe he was misinterpreting the moment.

Miles was about to tell himself, strike one. But he gave her the benefit of the doubt.

"I'm going into the city for an important meeting. It's a jeweler. I don't think it's a good idea—" Miles indicated by his disinterest that Bambi should hold off on any of her sudden passions. But then, to save Bambi's ego, he reached over and stroked her cheek.

At the same time he said, "But I'd love to do something later. Maybe at my place."

Bambi wanted to say, you mean your mother's place. But instead she said, "What about your moms?"

"She's gonna be at work," Miles replied with a smirk. Bambi smirked back, only not as convincing.

It was a busy Wednesday afternoon in midtown Manhattan. Tourists galore. Matinees thriving. Traffic controlling the pedestrians, and pedestrians controlling the traffic. Mayhem.

This was the third trip to the 47th Street "Diamond District" for Miles. On the crew's first prize, he cashed in with a local fence up near 241st Street in the Bronx. But Sonny knew better. His father had come into the city once upon a time, (long before the Marine Corps got a hold of him), to have his mother's wedding ring repaired. A diamond had come loose. And that exposure was all the suggestion Miles needed to see that the trip to 47th Street might bring better rewards; better than a local fence who dealt all kinds of sto-len goods. So, Miles went down and did his research. He browsed in the various shops with their brilliant glass dis-plays; cases filled with diamonds of every size. And he met with dozens of jewelers, hoping to find, perhaps, the most unscrupulous one. Someone who might sense that the jewels he brought in were stolen. But who wouldn't care either way.

"How much could I get for this?" Miles asked one jew-eler after the next. And he kept on asking until he found a set of eyes that were suspicious. Eyes that were desperate. Eyes that were smart—too smart just to be eyes.

"I don't know what last dealer offer you. But for risk I have to assume . . ." The man with dark gray hair and a sil-very, wrap-around beard spoke at low volume. His words came out chopped up.

"What risk? I already know this piece has twelve carats in it. I went to six dealers already."

"Yeah. But what they don't tell you is about security guard probably waiting to cuff you once deal is made and the au-thorities are called . . ." Miles couldn't make out the accent, but he could tell it was obviously foreign.

"They catch diamond thieves on this block at least four or five times a week."

"But—" Miles began to dispute the man's assumptions, and was interrupted.

"Listen, I'm not trying to make things hard. I want to make deal with you. I just want you to know the truth. Sasha Franco always tell truth."

Miles looked around, wondering if the dealer had al-ready pressed some hidden button behind the counter.

"So, what's the deal? What'll you give me?"

"Is this only piece?"

"No. I have a total of three pieces."

"You have them?"

"Yeah, but . . ."

"No problem. No need to show. Let me look this over once again."

Mr. Franco had a blazer and pants on, an olive & khaki

combo that went well with his sharp white shirt, bronze tie and gold cufflinks. He lifted up a magnifying glass to his eye to further inspect the catch.

"This piece I give you four if other pieces are same . . ."

"Four what?" Miles said indignantly, about to snatch the necklace from the older man and make a run for it. Four hundred? Hell no.

"Four thousand."

Miles was choked up. The fence would've said two, maybe three thousand at best.

"And if others are genuine, I give you equal. Cash. And more important, no police. No jail. Everything hush-hush."

Miles wanted to jump and shout. He wanted to click his heels. SCORE! But he had to maintain his composure. There were all sorts of distinguished jewelry dealers in this one venue where Sasha Franco was established. Something like a flea market for the wealthy. Heavily secured. Electronic surveillance. Curtained rooms for private viewings.

That was then. And now, Miles was back a 3rd time. He guessed the chains, medallions, the watch and earrings he and his boys roughed-off of the dude outside of the Shadow the night before to be worth at least $15,000 to $20,000. There was also a ring that even Miles could see had 10, maybe 15 diamonds in it.

As he waited for Mr. Franco, expecting nothing less than business-as-usual, cash on the nail, he gazed over to where Bambi was standing at another jeweler's glass showcase just a stone's throw away. Miles could see that the jeweler was pressing Bambi as a used car salesman would his only customer of the day. He got a kick out of seeing another man drool over his woman. And wasn't Bambi his woman. Didn't he have the greatest times of his life with her? Didn't she introduce him to ecstasy he'd never experienced before? And wasn't she a jewel herself? The finest he'd ever got his hands on?

Miles stood transfixed by Bambi's glow and how it reflected on others. Maybe there was a quirk or two in her

character. And so what. Didn't we all have our faults? And
didn't we strive to correct them whenever possible? All of
a sudden, Bambi was this stunning image. The diamond in
her hands cast rays that seemed to illuminate her, even creating an iridescent outline of her body. It was a sight to see,
like a breathtaking cloud before the sun. And Miles was
lured evermore. It startled the jeweler for Miles to slide up
behind Bambi as he did, to slip his arms around her and,
body to body, snuggle his lips into the back of her neck like
he did. If the salesman were a stack of building blocks, he'd
have fallen apart at that instant.

"I'm sorry, I didn't—" The guilty jeweler began to speak.

"Don't sweat it, buddy. I like other men goin' crazy over
my girl." Miles kissed Bambi again.

"Oooh, I like that," said Bambi in a bedroom-soft
voice.

The salesman was beet-red.

"Baby, what do you think about this?" Bambi had on a
diamond ring that sparkled against her Snicker bar-brown
skin.

"I like, I like. How about we put a down payment on
that."

Miles heard himself say this, but couldn't believe it himself. What was he saying?

"But this is too big for a friendship ring . . ."

Bambi's words were suspended as Miles covered her
mouth with his. It was a sensual kiss that meant so much
more than any other they shared since their first kiss.

"I wasn't thinking about a friendship ring, I was talking
about an engagement ring."

Bambi stood there with her mouth open, as if her face
was caught in a deep freeze.

"Oh my G—od!"

Bambi lunged into Miles, her arms taking in as much of
him as she could. Miles enjoyed the attention. He was happy
to bring Bambi joy, whatever it took. Wasn't that love? Giving? Committing? At that point it didn't matter about preparing for the moment or any kind of formal, get-on-your-knees

type of conviction. Miles wanted Bambi. Bambi wanted Miles. Soulmates forever.

Miles had to shake himself away from the fever that he had caused. Bambi gave the ring on her finger a more possessive look and discussed some other things about its contents with the jeweler. Meanwhile, Miles backed off, knowing he had business to attend to. Where was Mr. Franco anyway?

Back at Franco's, Miles realized how high he was, considering the windfall of cash he was about to receive. Sure the idea of money, of convenience, and that there was more where that came from helped to fuel his commitment to Bambi. But so what. That was young love. How many rich executives are promoted to CEO or president, only to dive deeper into the game of life with all its risks and consequences? Why should ghetto love be any different?

Miles was tired of wondering, of thinking. Where was Mr. Franco?

"Miles."

"*Damn*, it's about time," Miles exhaled.

"Would you step back with me?"

Miles didn't want to make sense of the request. It had to be the amount of money he'd be taking home. Maybe a necessary security measure.

"What's up?"

"I want you look in glass."

Sasha Franco had a small office behind his curtain. The diamonds were there on a desk under a bright lamp that reached over from end of an elbow.

"What am I looking for?" Miles asked.

"The top stone is called the table."

"Okay."

"Now look at ring next over."

Sasha replaced the first ring with another.

"Look at table now."

Miles took a second or two, but couldn't see anything special.

"I don't get it."

"Change ring again," Sasha said.

And Miles repeated the switch. Then again.

"Okay, one table is fuller and one has more sparkle."

"Good. Now guess which one is not diamond."

"Not diamond?"

Miles stretched his eyelids in that instant, not ready for a disappointment.

"This one?"

Miles pointed out the wrong diamond. But Sasha picked up the ring that Miles brought him. He was wagging his head.

"The only real diamonds are the earrings. The ring? Falsch . . ."

Sasha had a small wooden hammer in his hand with the ring positioned on the edge of the desk. He brought the hammer down and smashed the ring.

"FALSCH," he said.

Then he put the watch in the same spot. Again with the hammer.

"COPYCAT!"

Now Sasha took a medallion and squeezed it into a vise grip. He reached for a pair of pliers. Miles winced as the jeweler bent the medallion until it snapped in half.

"This? Costume jewelry."

Miles took a much needed deep breath.

"What about the earrings?" Miles braced himself.

"One set of earrings . . . good. Two carats. Out of sympathy I give you two thousand."

Miles quickly calculated the cut he'd get. About $650. He'd promised his moms $300. His cell phone bill was $200. The gas tank was on "E" and Bambi was out there praising that twelve thousand-dollar rock as if it were her own.

CHAPTER FIVE

"Sonny. Sonny, wake up." Charlene, Sonny's sister, was nudging him out of his deep sleep the morning after the heist.

"Come on, it's gettin' past noon, and you promised to take me to the Westchester. Come on."

She gave him another good shove. He wasn't gonna weasel out of this promise.

"Alright. Alright. Ease up sis, damn. What time is it?"

"I just said, it's gettin' past noon. Now you know this is my last day home. I gotta get back to the base before oh-seven-hundred tomorrow."

Sonny hated that, how Charlene kept up with that military lingo around him. Couldn't she be more sensitive, considering that he failed to make it through boot camp? Considering that she achieved and completed what he couldn't?

"Chill sis, chill. I'm up. Gimme five minutes."

Sonny had been dreaming that Miles showed up at his doorstep with an armored car parked out in front of the house.

"Where you want it parked?"

"Huh?" Sonny had said, not yet fully awake.

"The truck, man. Where you want it?"

"Come on dog. Quit with the jokes. I didn't have break-fast yet." And that's when Sonny about shut the door in his comrade's face. But Miles pushed the door back open.

"Sonny, wake the fuck up. I got you piece of the money."

"In that?" Sonny gazed over Miles's shoulder. *"Damn, dog. How much did we get?"*

"Two mill each."

"Two mill? As in million?"

"No as in pennies. Yes, fool-ass niggah."

"How'd you do that?" asked Sonny.

"One of the rings Matchstick had was laced with precious stones. Don't ask me. Franco just paid up. Just like usual."

"Well goooooo-damn!"

The Brink's truck had already backed into the driveway with the two diamond thieves offloading bags of money when Charlene woke Sonny, the dreamer. As he got dressed he imagined Miles already down on 47th, already leaving Sasha Franco with a bag of money, or at least with his pockets full of big-faced bills. So, in his mind, half of the dream had already come true.

In the meantime, he had promised to take his sister shopping at the Westchester, the high-priced mall up in White Plains. No, Sonny didn't have his piece of the prize money yet, but that was no matter. He was sure that Miles would come through as he had all other times in the past.

Charlene had a rental car which she drove up from Camp Legune, North Carolina, (where she was stationed), and she wasted no time whisking Sonny off to the mall.

"Sonny, whatcha be doin' late at night?"

"Whatchu talkin' about, girl?"

"I'm talkin' about you sneakin' off with the Benz at all hours of the night. Don't play a playa, Sonny."

Sonny sucked his teeth. Convicted. Then he said, "Ain't shit. Just hangin' out with some of my boys."

"Some of your boys," Charlene repeated without any added emotion. "And what do you and your boys do with no jobs, no money and Ma's car."

"If I didn't have no money, why am I takin' you shoppin'?"

Charlene couldn't argue that point. She simply said, "I

just don't want to see you in no trouble, dude. You are my only brother."

"Yes, Major General Stewart." Sonny made a half-assed salute. "Now, stop by the ATM, Charlene. I gotta get some dough."

At the machine Sonny blocked his sister's view just in case she was being nosey. Again. The screen read $400. Sonny took $380. Tomorrow he'd deposit six or seven hundred to keep it open. The rest of his cut he'd put between his mattresses.

Charlene felt a special union between her and Sonny. They were just a year apart, him being the youngest. And they did mostly everything together. He played basketball in high school, and so did she. He was a camp counselor during his summers off, so was she. They both earned their driver's license together, double dated other brother-sister duos, and even shared some of the same jeans and sweatshirts. They even looked like twins. Charlene went into basic training a year before Sonny, and the Marine Corps didn't make it much easier for her, being a woman and all. However, Charlene stuck it out. She persevered. She was relentless about what she wanted.

Sonny went to Parris Island with all the same intentions. But it was tougher for him. That Drill instructor Thorton. Shit. He fucked up Sonny's dream. Made it into a nightmare overnight. Sonny heard about this guy Thorton, too. He even said a silent prayer before training, hoping that he wouldn't face him. But the prayer wasn't heard. Thorton picked at Sonny as if there was a "fuck with me" label affixed to his forehead. Everything from taking ice cold showers, to then doing pushups butt naked with the windows open to October's chill. Everything from turning the other recruits against Sonny, to eventually referring him for a disciplinary discharge. Sergeant Thorton essentially changed Sonny's life. His relationship was never the same with his sister Charlene after the discharge. Life was never more miserable in general. In the belly of his consciousness Sonny Stewart hated all-things-military and all-things government. He didn't want a job. He didn't want college, and he didn't have the wherewithal to start his own business. Sonny felt like a liability. His parents were successful. His sister was successful. But he was a failure. So if life wouldn't afford him an equal shot at opportunity then Sonny was left to do one thing. He had to take what he wanted.

When Sonny got back in the car Charlene asked him, "How is Dori? You still seein' her?"

"Hmmm, why is it that every damn girl from around the way gotta try-n-be Whitney Houston, Janet Jackson or the new Aaliyah? I got a friend, and his girl wants the same dammed thing. Like somebody's gonna notice them over the forty million other wannabees out there . . . man." Sonny was referring to Miles and his girlfriend Bambi. "If these shorties would just get a life and stop chasin' some pie-in-the-sky dream . . ."

"Like you did? No, don't even look at me crazy, Sonny. There was a time that you wanted to be an NBA player. Then you said you'd do twenty years in the Corps and replace Colin Powell as President. Who's the one who needs to get a life?"

"You got a lotta nerve, sis and I'm takin' *you* shoppin'?"

"One thing ain't never gonna change between me n' you Sonny. I'm always gonna keep it real with you. I'm always gonna tell you what's in my heart. And right now . . . I miss my brother." A tear welled up in Charlene's eye, but she wouldn't let it fall. She'd come too far to submit to emotion. If Sonny didn't keep a backbone, at least she would. "I hope you find your way Sonny. In my heart I pray you succeed."

"Thanks sis. I will. You'll see."

Sonny spent every dime on Charlene already cute with her natural look and smiling eyes, wanting to wrap his sister in the best civilian clothes his money could buy. Charlene was too flattered to care where this money was coming from. After all, he did get it out of the ATM, didn't he? Then *of course* that money was his. Of course it was legit. Why second guess what seemed obvious?

On Sunday he kissed Charlene on the cheek and she was off on her drive back to the base. She'd be a Corporal soon. Sonny made a mental note to set something aside to celebrate her new rank. Then he jumped on the Metro North train at the White Plains train station. In 30 minutes he'd meet up with Gus and Miles at Grand Central Station.

CHAPTER SIX

Gus Chambers could do no wrong. He finally got up enough dough to buy the Pathfinder truck, and now, as soon as Miles showed up, he'd be over the top. Enough to get the scar under his eye "fixed." He'd checked with a plastic surgeon as soon as last week and found that the cost would be $4000. Surely, Miles would have more than that for him. The new ride, the scar, and also his own apartment . . . Gus knew he had it all. And as far as he could see there was no end in sight. Even though he didn't have a millionaire's wealth he felt like a million dollars. As though there was a money tree available to him exclusively.

This was the highlight of Gus' life. He never came by so much money so easily. Not only that, Gus could claim Miles and Sonny as his family, where otherwise he'd have none. The Marine Corps had been his only hope after his pops was convicted in a drug conspiracy. Then the feds had come to take all the household appliances. Eventually, they confiscated the house as well. Gus was forced to make desperate decisions. Since he was only 17, he forged his pop's signature where parental consent was required. Not long thereafter, past the physical, the basic I.Q. test and a half dozen orientation videos, Gus was on the bus headed (they said) for hell.

Gus and Miles happened to be on that same Greyhound, even though Gus was recruited in the Bronx and Miles in

Yonkers. They didn't get to know each other however until the first week of boot camp. They were tight ever since. At the rifle range on Parris Island there was a rule. Keep your M-16 pointed forward or up to the sky. But Miles was having issues. A round had gotten stuck in this rifle and it jammed him up. It frustrated him. He'd just managed to get a rhythm going, first missing his target completely. But by the tenth and eleventh rounds Miles was hitting the half-dollar-sized black dot again and again. From 50 yards away, the bullseye was nearly ripped from the center of his target sheet. That's when the shit jammed. Feverish and wanting to get back on track from his spread-eagle position on the firing line, Miles curled up slightly and pulled in the weapon to check the magazine. There were three drill instructors on duty at the time, two of whom had been with Platoon 3002 since day one. The other was specifically assigned to the rifle range, assisting one platoon after another as they spent Stage Two learning marksmanship. Gus was four or five recruits to the left of Miles, only coming close to hitting the bull's-eye. He didn't realize Miles was having problems until the outburst of shouting. All at once, three drill instructors were standing over Miles, cursing, spitting and red eyed. The gunfire blasts suddenly faded to deathly silence.

"YOU STUPID MOTHERFUCKER! YOU DON'T KNOW THE RULES? YOU DON'T KNOW THE FUCKING RULES."

"GET UP!!! GET THE FUCK UP YOU BEADY-EYED ASSHOLE."

"TEN-HUT MOTHER FUCKER! TEN-HUT!

Miles was up on his feet, rifle at his side, standing at attention.

"PRESENT ARMS! PRESENT ARMS!!!"

Miles lifted the M-16 for the drill instructor to accept. But the Gunny Sergeant in charge of the rifle range was already snatching it from his hands. At the same time Sergeant Thorton and Gracie were shouting at Miles, close enough to bite his ears off.

"GET ON THE FUCKING GROUND AND GIMME FIFTY!" Thor yelled.

"GET UP!! GET THE FUCK UP!!!" another yelled.

"GET DOWN . . . IN THE DIRT. LAY IT DOWN!"

The DIs had Miles petrified before he submitted to their storm of direct orders. Then he turned into somewhat of an acrobat as he jumped from one order to the next, all the while breaking a sweat and struggling to breathe. The assault didn't let up. The drill instructors sought to make an example of Miles.

"STAND UP STRAIGHT BOY!!! DO IT!! RUN IN PLACE! STOP! ON YOUR STOMACH! STOP! ON YOUR BACK!! UP ON YOUR FEET!!"

In the meantime Gus was hyperventilating and taking every bit of this personally. He watched with pent up rage as the attack took a toll on his friend. There was a point when Miles couldn't move any longer. He was fatigued and exhausted. He'd given up. They were breaking him. As Miles stood there slouched with his head sunk down below his shoulders, Sergeant Thorton swung an open hand, slapping Miles hard enough to send him to the ground.

The drill instructors were quickly surprised. All 6'0 and 195lbs of Gus was charging at them like a winged linebacker, with his head and body angled like a lightning bolt, leaning in forward and closing the gap until the confusion of bodies thudded to the ground. Within hours, both Miles Green and Gus chambers were reassigned to the military discharge unit where they waited with dozens of others for a Greyhound bus to take them back home. Sonny was already there, ejected from Thorton's previous platoon. But once the three realized they were all neighbors (Gus from the Bronx, Sonny from White Plains, and Miles from Yonkers), an instant bond was born. They spoke of their destroyed hopes and their families' inevitable disappointment. They recalled traces of resources left back home. What would they do now? What was life gonna be like now? How would the world look at them? Wasn't a dishonorable discharge like a criminal record? Since they were marked men, was there anything left to lose?

* * *

Now came the rendezvous where the three diamond bandits were to meet and divvy up the proceeds of the catch. Gus and Sonny were waiting on Miles, both of them jumping to conclusions.

"Come on man, don't be like that. This is Miles you talkin' about. Not just any nigga off the block. I trust that ma-fucka with my life."

"I just hope you trust him with our money," Sonny replied, a little concerned because so much money was expected.

"Don't worry so much, man. We a team. We got a lot left to do, more money comin' down the road than this you worryin' about."

Sonny's eyes reconciled. Gus was sure right about that.

Come on Miles. At least hit my pager, dog. Gus was having his own hint of doubt as the two stood there by the information booth at the center of Grand Central main concourse. Both of them panning left and right towards the terminal's many entrances and exits, its walkways and corridors, its mass of travelers, hucksters and homeless.

Miles wasn't alone when he arrived. And he was more than 20 minutes late, which was unlike him. All three agreed on timeliness in addition to honor, discipline and duty as traits that they'd keep and stick to. These were some of the things they learned in training; things that it didn't take common sense to understand or adhere to.

"Damn, dog. What was you, like, printin' the money?" Gus asked, half joking.

Miles rolled his eyes, expressing that he'd been to Hell and back. Then he said, "We gotta talk. But before I forget, this is Elvis Evans. Elvis, this is my man Gus Chambers, we were in Three Thousand Two together . . . and this is my man Sonny, the dude I told you came home with us."

They shook hands and found a quiet corner on the upper level of a McDonald's restaurant a block away. Amidst a table full of fries, burgers and drinks, all which Elvis paid for, Miles dropped the bombs.

"I got good news and bad news. First, the bad news. The thing we did the other night came up zero."

"Zero?" Both Sonny and Gus spoke at the same time.

"Well, maybe not exactly zero." Miles took prearranged folds of money and handed them to his partners. The money was quickly counted.

"Seven hundred?" Sonny said, visibly distraught.

"Dude musta' been a phony baller, 'cause most of his shit was phony. Sasha broke a few pieces right in front of me . . . used a wooden hammer too. Said they was false."

"So Sasha gave you cash for the broken stuff?"

"Naw. He said one set of earrings was legit. But I think he felt bad for us. He came up with two gees."

"So this is the good news?" Sonny asked, indicating the money in his hand. He and Gus were still numb from the bad news.

"Naw. Elvis here is the good news. You're gonna trip about this coincidence, but it's like this: Elvis was in Platoon Three Thousand down on Parris Island. Just a few months before the rest of us. And guess who his drill instructor was?"

"No shit. Thor?"

"You got it."

"Man, just hearin' his name, I wanna smack the shit out of his moms for openin' her legs to his pops."

"Damn Gus. I thought you was over that."

"Naw. Everyday I look in the mirror, everyday I see this scar on my face I think of murderin' that motherfucka." All of them were silent, wanting to let that be.

"So tell us more about this good news Miles," said Sonny.

"I'll let Elvis tell it."

Now everyone looked at Elvis. Not dark enough to be called black, not light enough to be called white, Elvis couldn't be older than 25.

"When I met Miles and we got to talkin', I found out we all have a lot in common. How we got jacked by the Marine Corps . . . our situations with comin' home . . . tryin' to make sense of this world. Plus, I joined up with the grimy side myself. I had to do a few B and E's, I hit a few convenience stores, but then I met up with this dude named Rose. Real thorough cat from Harlem. I broker gun deals for him. It brings me good money, but nothin' like what y'all are into."

"So remember what you said about strappin' up Sonny? Well, this is the man. Plus Elvis, tell 'em what you told me."

"Okay, there's this rapper I know, he's phony as shit, but his diamonds are real. He came to me for a nine—said he needed to protect his jewels, said he spent his whole advance from his second album, one hundred thousand dollars, on diamonds and a pimped-out Cadillac Escalade. I seen his last video. It went to number one on that BET show, *One-O-Six Park*. He wears the shit in videos, on the street . . . everywhere. He talks all that mess in his music-n-shit, but he always rides with one or two security dudes."

Sonny did the calculations. The partners never did a hit that made them so much as $20,000 or $30,000 each. And with the Matchstick heist going belly-up, the rapper move sounded like candy.

Gus thought briefly about the rapper Elvis spoke of, recalling a music video that stayed at number one for a week and a half. "GET AT ME I'M RIGHT UP IN YOUR FACE / I'M THE ONE WITH THE ROLEX WRIST, AND ICE THAT BLINDS THE PLACE . . . GET AT ME, AIN'T NO NEED FOR ME TO HIDE / YOU MIGHT FIND ME CHILLIN ON THE AVE, OR IN MY TRICKED-OUT RIDE." Now that Elvis said the rapper was "a phony", it sparked some opinions that Gus also had. It was easy to conjure hate for someone he didn't even know, who he never ever met. Perhaps Gus, Sonny and Miles needed such an opportunity, a person towards whom they could direct their own hostilities while making some money in the meantime. And now, Elvis was handing them that very opportunity on a silver platter.

"So what's gonna make this particular job easier than what we're used to?"

"Besides the hundred thousand dollars in diamonds?" Elvis said this as if that was reason enough. Then he said, "Because I have exclusive information about a specific individual who will be vulnerable at a specific place and time. Because I can be an asset to you, make us a nice piece of change. *Quick*."

Miles jumped in to say, "The loss we took on the Matchstick deal is peanuts compared to this. We'll be able to see that as a lesson learned—not a tragedy or a loss. We'll be able to move on."

All of this was hitting Sonny and Gus like a thousand gallons of water at once. One moment they're struck with the news about the phony jewels, and the next they're concerned about this stranger, Elvis (Was he still alive?), who knew all about their dirt. Now Miles was endorsing Elvis and (did they hear this guy correctly?) his proposal for an overnight hundred thousand dollar heist.

Without question it was time for a group discussion before anyone did anything.

Mrs. Green was very nice these days, allowing Miles to use the Pontiac just about as much as he wanted to. After all, he had been giving her a few dollars here and there; he'd paid good money too for new tires and to have the brakes redone. And just yesterday he came through with the $300 he promised her. There it was again, money, making everything all nicey nicey.

And now that Miles and his soldiers were executing this profitable operation, and in effect raking in the dough, what they were involved in could very well be perceived as a company. The Pontiac conveniently became their company car.

"I just wanna know what kind of asset Elvis will be," Sonny was saying this as the three were knee-deep into the Elvis-for-hire discussion. "I mean, so what if the rapper-cat got diamonds. I bet there's a hundred or a thousand rappers out in the world. Probably got their phone numbers and address listed, too."

"Okay Sonny, I'm hearin' you on that. But I want you to remember somethin' Elvis said, he said he's just like us. He learned what we learned. He learned how to kill, to cut a man's heart out, to shoot like a pro. Sonny, the guy had the same goddamned drill instructor we had went through the bullshit with Thor. He's angry. He's hungry, and he's dedicated. We gotta respect that."

"But a name like Elvis?" Gus said with a chuckle. "It gotta make you wonder if all his screws is tight."

"Gus, Sonny, get past the bullshit. Recognize one thing. He's down to help us get to the big money. We all want that. We don't wanna be doin' this for the rest of our lives. You want your clothing store, and Gus, you want that car and that townhouse. I wanna marry Bambi. We all want something. So why wait? Let's use Elvis's help, get what's ours to take, and move on with our goals."

There was no argument. They realized that this was a step up to the next level. Destiny was calling out for them. Good or bad.

Miles stopped to pick up Elvis and the four of them took the hour-long drive to Staten Island. There was a video shoot for Bling, the rapper who shamelessly flaunted his jewels and who made millions (or so it seemed) from rapping about those same jewels. His lyrics, *the source* said, were all about nothin', yet nobody could explain it. How could this guy sell a million CD's?

CHAPTER SEVEN

The parking lot out in back of the Green Acre's Mall was converted into a music video set. Two private security cars, each with one rent-a-cop, were parked so as to seal-off the entrance and exit of the lot. Four large trailers and a tour bus were parked adjacent to the trailers as background for the video. Behind the expensive vehicles was a 30-foot curtain of black canvas draped from high-wire cables. Scattered betwixt and between the equipment, the maze of cables, the trailers and the tour bus were various cars and jeeps belonging to various hangers-on, family and friends of the rapper known as Bling.

By now plenty of video footage had already been recorded of the 10 cocoa-brown cuties; all of them babes-for-hire in pink or white micro-mini skirts, hot shorts and stiletto ankle boots, and grinding, hugging and kissing up on Bling as he pretended to be hard and unimpressed inside one of the limos. The 2nd half of the video shoot, including shots of the girls rubbing up against the golden Land Rovers, had to wait till nightfall so that the gold, pink, white and all the jewels which Bling wore would stand out brilliantly against the jet black atmosphere.

    This (some would think) was the life.

* * *

The past 5 years of this life, Bling's life, was set up. Fabricated. Designed to win over the music industry. First of all, the Queens-born-and-raised rapper had to be relocated to Atlanta, where radio stations (unlike New York and LA) regularly gave airplay to local acts. Everybody was familiar with how Master P, Ludacris and Cash Money hit big in their localities long before signing with major labels and national distribution. So since the south was hot, it made perfect sense to think ahead and set up house in the "ATL." Financing wasn't a problem. Bling's backer was his notorious numbers-running brother Bingo. Bingo made it convenient and feasible for Bling's high profile lifestyle (the clothes and jewels), the initial production of the music, the CD pressings, radio ad buys and even the hotel stays during his promo tour.

All the work paid off. The 1st album went triple platinum, 3 million. But Bling's fame dried up after a while. The music industry called his success bogus after it was all said and done. After they'd already fell for the smoke and mirrors, hook, line and sinker.

But now Bling was on the comeback, trying to push the flash, money and jewels until he could ride the wave no more. And even Bingo played a bigger role now, setting up larger payoffs.

He approached the network of the street vendors and supplied them with a bootleg copy of the 2nd album behind the back of the record label. Before long, it was time to make the impression on radio. Lance Holiday at WKLA-Los Angeles endorsed Bling's single "GET AT ME!" saying, "Any song I can play 20 times in a row in my truck and still wanna play it some more has gotta be a smash hit!"

Fat Lisa from WHST-Houston said, *"Great track! Dope lyrics! This new Bling joint has HIT written all over it!"* Shoop G from WZEE-Tennessee told *Billboard Magazine*, *"I can't stop playing it!"* And Shoop G was telling the truth. It was the day he told Bling Records, *"No"* and *"the record was some garbage,"* that he received a visit from two thugs with bandanas and bad attitudes. By the time the visit was over, Shoop G was wearing a "Bling!" bandana himself and his attitude had done a 360° degree turnaround. Hip Hop was an ugly, ruthless industry. And if you had money, you were winning. In some cases, by any means necessary.

Inside of the tour bus, a complete lap of luxury, Bling's publicist was fielding calls from hype surrounding "GET AT ME!" The bus was busy with 2 Bling reps, five family members, a writer and photographer from XXL and some of the babes from the video. Bling was laid back with two of the girls, making small talk, waving off a signal to cut short the XXL interview. All of this after he'd just been crisscrossing the country (again) for the past 3 weeks as part of his 2 month promotional tour for the new album. He did the local retail outlets, he performed at small venues, and he pressed flesh and politicked with any and everyone. Bling's publicist was working double-time to get his face everywhere. Strewn about the bus were Bling bandanas and posters. CD's and magazines.

"We're going to need a really big push before his album drops," the publicist was saying into the phone while her eye and free ear still hustled to keep abreast of the XXL reporter with Bling. "I want as many of the local and regional urban mags, websites and cable shows as we can get our teeth into. And tell that West Coast street team that we will not be responsible for municipal fines this go 'round. Tell 'em to stay off the telephone poles, stick to trees and bus stops."

Meanwhile, across from the publicist, the reporter asked Bling, "How would you define your magnetism?"

"You really gotta ask my peoples that . . . they the best judges, right ladies?" The two women at his sides, obedient as molten chocolate, snuggled up and affirmed whatever Bling wanted. "But to keep it real wit' you," Bling added, "I think heads are mostly checkin' for DMX, Jay-Z and that Eminem cat. I'm surprised people even smell me."

The publicist tried to avoid rolling her eyes, having heard

Bling's humble address from a distance for the umpteenth time.

Just then . . . the bus jerked, sending a jolt through everyone on board. Confusion masked every face. The bus was moving? Oh shit!

"Hey! Hey driver!"

The shouts were an immediate response. The publicist was the first one to jump up, and she trotted to the front to see the driver.

"Hi there sweetie," the stranger said from beside the driver. "Didn't mean to shake you up . . ."

"Where's the bus going?"

"Oh, a little trip. Nothing to be overly concerned about. But . . ." The man put his finger to his temple thinking about something. "What you can do is put your hands on your head and keep your mouth shut." Elvis pulled down his ski mask and took the cell phone from her.

Elvis felt as if he was going a bit far, sticking two loaded M-1 pistols in the face of this pony-tailed publicist with the captivating baby blue eyes. She was less than harmless, and more than scared to death. But this was a hundred thousand dollar operation here. Nothing less important than robbing a major downtown bank. They'd have to be alert, they'd have to be quick, and they couldn't take anything for granted. Not even the fragile publicist.

"This is not a game. I said put your hands on your head."

To show he meant business, Elvis brought one of the pistols down and pointed it at her genitalia. The hands shot up with life-or-death quickness.

"Now I want you to sit here and when the bus pulls up to the security guards, tell them there's something important Bling wants to see to. Tell them you'll be back and that there's no need for alarm."

Elvis gestured to Gus, letting him know to keep the bus driver under the gun, and Sonny joined Miles, heading towards the rear of the bus, both with loaded weapons. All of them now with their ski masks lowered. Elvis fired his weapon into the publicist's abandoned laptop computer, out of anyone's harm.

"Okay folks, this is the story. We're gonna take a short ride."

The computer's short circuiting was of little consequence amidst the screams and fear filling the suddenly tight atmosphere inside the bus.

"As soon as we clear the lot you's gonna step up one at a time towards the front of the bus . . ."

Miles and Sonny began counting heads, while Elvis maintained the threat of mortal danger, his M-1 pistols swiveling back and forth, not missing a soul with his aim.

"Before you step up, you're going to loosen up your clothing. That means shirt buttons, snaps, zippers and belt buckles."

There was a consistence of questioning expressions throughout the small group of 15. Wonder mixed with fear, mixed with desperation. The bus came to a halt at the exit of the parking lot. The gunmen compelled the prisoners to hush up, letting them know that they'd stay alive as long as they cooperated. For a short time there was silence. Some voiced their wishes for clear passage, while others prayed for help. The wait was tense. Sonny, Elvis and Miles simultaneously imagined the rent-a-cop's curiosity, his inquiry, and then ultimately his absence of choice. Then the bus rolled forward again. A combination of exhales was released all at once, as gravity and movement pushed and pulled at their bodies.

"Okay ladies and gentlemen, get with the undoing of the clothes."

"This is crazy," someone said further back, but neither Miles, Sonny or Elvis could tell who it was.

"Who said that shit? Who said it? Step up, or we'll start droppin' you one by one in this mothafucka."

"Me . . . I said it." A man stepped forward. He was bespeckled, broad shouldered with a goatee and an inch-high

crew cut. He had a proud red expression on his face. It was
the XXL reporter.

"Hero, huh?"

"It's not that, I just—"

Sonny cut the explanation before it turned into a speech,
swinging the gun he had so that it connected with Mr. XXL's
cheek. The man crashed backwards onto the couch where
Bling and the dancers sat dumbfounded.

"Now. Anybody *else* got somethin' slick to say out their
mouth?"

Not a peep, just the rumble of the motor as the bus cruised
away from the mall.

"Good. Then I'll start with you. Start with putting that
camera right here in the bag. Then come up off that watch,
your wallet . . . cash. All your shit. LET'S GO! I ain't got all
day." Sonny the commander.

"You," said Elvis to a woman who was dressed like she
was going to church. She had on an ivory silk tunic with
floral designs, matching rayon pants, earrings and a bracelet. It seemed that she had made herself at home on the bus
considering her shoes were off. Her hair was done up in a
twist with a few bangs hanging over her forehead. The woman's swollen features, her wide nostrils, thick eyelids, cheeks
and large teeth under the broad lips all made her look to be
50 years of age.

"Young man I don't know what you're thinking but—"

"Cut the speech, moms Mabley. I don't discriminate. Now
take off them earrings, that bracelet, and drop 'em in the bag."

The woman looked appalled, but followed orders. Meanwhile, Miles kept an eye on his companions, even as Bling
took his arms from around the frightened video chicks, apparently with some intention of defending the woman.

"Hey, that's my aunt."

"She shoulda stayed home," Elvis answered with a quickness. "And don't worry, we'll be gettin' at you shortly." Meanwhile, Miles curled his finger at a young girl who looked to
be about 5 years old. Obediently, the child stepped forth

before her mother could object. Miles flashed the child's mother a compassionate eye, to hopefully console her.

"What's your name?" Miles asked.

"Kameka," the girl said sweetly, and hesitantly.

"Okay Kameka, we're going through a little rehearsal here for the video okay?"

"Den' how come you got guns?" the child asked, twisting a lock of her hair as she spoke.

"It's, uh, part of the video."

"No it's not. This a *robbery*." The child's brows furrowed.

"O-kay. You're a little wiser than I thought. But I want you to be safe, so go to the back of the bus and lock yourself in the bathroom . . . cool?"

"What-ever," the girl made a sassy face and spun away, rushing past her mother in the quest to save her own ass. Now Miles signaled the little girl's mother.

"I'm gonna let you go in the bathroom with your lil' girl . . . *wait*. Ah-ah-ah, I'm not through with you." Miles used the finger gesture pulling at her.

"You know the routine," he said with the steely gaze. "You gotta empty your purse, too."

Buck was just a little pissed right now. Two hundred pounds of mostly muscles, three years working for Bling as head of security and handy with the 9 millimeter strapped to his leg, and still these thugs were able to get at him.

Buck was rubbing the lumps at the rear of his scalp now, not at all impressed with the tinge of pain back there. When he came to his senses he realized that he was in the back seat of some car, probably carried there by the three (or was it four?) dudes who rushed him. Scrambling to an upright position, Buck immediately realized the emergency. The tour bus was gone!

"Anybody seen Nitro? HAS ANYBODY SEEN NI-TRO!!?" Buck was out of the car, standing between the trailers and the flashy stretch Range Rovers, yelling at the top of his lungs, thugged out with denim jacket and multi-pocket cargo pants, Timberland boots and a do rag. He realized his diamond crucifix was missing and took off sprinting amidst a few dozen puzzled video crewmembers and extras. The rent-a-cop was already standing outside of the red and white Dodge at the exit of the mall parking lot, watching anxiously as Buck approached.

"What's wrong?" he asked, reading the distress on Buck's face.

"The bus! Which way did it go?"

"Towards the expressway," the uniformed security said. Buck was already opening the passenger-side door of the Dodge. "Come on. We gotta catch 'em." When they were both in the car racing in the direction of the bus, Buck asked, "Got a cell phone?" "Nope. But, er . . . I got this here two-way. Patrol two to base. Patrol two to base, come in!" The radio speaker squealed as the two beckoned for a response.

"Patrol two, come in base!" The rent-a-cop might've gotten a laugh out of Buck under different circumstances, what with how he looked like a character out of a cartoon and all. The puffy cheeks, the tiny eyes and overwhelming forehead was as close to Popeye's as Buck had ever seen.

"It's no use. I don't think this operates more'n a block away from the mall." The guy sounded like a raspy 50 year old. Buck rolled his eyes, sat back and rested his cheek against the ball of his palm.

"This shit is crazy. Right out of the blue these idiots come and fuck up my record?"

"You's all were makin' a video and a record?" Buck turned to the rent-a-cop, not believing what he'd heard.

"Don't you see what's goin' on here? Somebody hijacked the tour bus! The performer, his family, people from the record label . . ."

"Jeez. They hijacked the record labels?" guessed the rent-a-cop.

The comment made Buck look away from the man, knowing that he wouldn't say one more word to him. If he did, and if this fool said one more stupid thing, there might be a strangling to go with the kidnapping and robbery.

From about 300 yards Buck spotted the back of the bus

as it turned left onto a street traveling parallel to the Long Island Expressway.

"There! It's making a right! Hurry!!"

The old man pressed down into the accelerator like he'd just been given license to speed. The rent-a-cop turned road dog.

"Hold it! Stop. Stop!" Buck could feel himself pushing his foot into the floor of the car, as though he had control of the brakes. The car hadn't even come to a full halt before Buck jumped out. "NITRO!" Buck recognized him the moment the Dodge hit the turn. Nitro was his partner. They lifted weights together. They both worked as Bling's private security for the past three years, and quiet as it was kept, they were lovers, too. "You alright, boo?" Nitro grunted, dazed by the toss he'd just taken. "Man, they took the bus, Buck. I didn't see you; but when I looked in the front where the driver was there were like some dudes up in there who I didn't know. So I ran up and hung on."

"You were hanging on the back of the bus?"

"I know, I know, crazy huh?" Nitro with the shame. And then Buck took a second look at Nitro. "Are you okay? Anything broken?"

"I don't think so. My arm is bruised pretty bad." Nitro's eyes beckoned for attention, both physical and mental.

"Oh boobie, daddy'll take care-a that."

"Hey! Ya'll better hurry on if ya' want to catch that bus. They sure is movin' fast."

"Come on Nitro. Lemme' help you in the car. We gotta catch up to Bling. That's our bread 'n butter they stealin'." Buck and Nitro, the queer bodyguards.

The Dodge picked up speed once again, a bit more weight in motion now with four hundred pounds of muscle, one old geezer and a pinch of lilac.

"We got company," Gus said, stepping back some where most of the others were congregated in the bus. "That rent-a-cop is comin' up behind us." Gus waited a second, anticipating some kind of directive. The bus began to smell of flesh, the scent of too many folks perspiring within one small space. Miles nodded at Gus, a look that said he'd see to the problem. Gus widened his eyes at the sight of all those bodies back there, many of the passengers stripped down to their intimate apparel.

"Okay, speed it up," Miles told the rapper's uncle. The man with the receding hairline, an outdated three-piece Easter suit and a pipe that reminded Miles of Sherlock Holmes. Already Miles could see the man was gonna have a time with the disrobing.

Meanwhile Sonny was attending to one of the video chicks that had been sitting aside of Bling. This, he couldn't wait for. The girl had to be nineteen, twenty at best and Sonny was carrying a bold, chauvinistic demeanor, but for down deep his loins were curling up into his stomach. She didn't have much to take off, already dressed in tight hot pants, a bikini top and the stiletto boots. Sonny turned his lips to conceal his licking them as he watched her bend down to undo her ankle bracelet.

"My brother gave me this," she said on the verge of tears.

"You on the wrong side of the game, baby. You know these rapper cats is just pimpin' you in they videos, actin' like they take you home-n-all . . ."

The dancer sucked her teeth. "You need to come-n-get with a real nigga, a nigga who's gonna treat you right." Sonny Stewart, Mr. Congeniality. The dancer made a face that said "fat chance." That turned Sonny off. "Whatever," he said. "Just get the pants off. I got plans for you."

"But I don't have any on."

"Did I ask you?" Sonny with the gun to the dancer's temple.

"Don't go crazy, son," said Miles, not wanting to use Sonny's name in full. "Just the valuables, and stick with the plan."

"I am," Sonny replied. "The bitch ain't got draws on. What I'm supposed to do?"

Before Miles or Sonny could decide on what to do about

this, the girl already took down her tight shorts. The sight mesmerized the gunmen. She had herself shaved till it left a thinned out heart shaped patch of pubic hair. Bling hadn't even gotten this far with her.

Trying to maintain his composure, Sonny told the girl to take off her bracelet and necklace, too. Her bangled earrings were already in the bag.

Elvis had stepped over to speak confidentially to Miles and the two came up with a snap decision.

"Okay, here's the rest of the story," Elvis announced. Miles had already made his way up to the driver's area, looking out through the side view mirror.

"Driver, I want you to slow up when I say the word. Somethin' like 5 miles per hour—you got that?"

"Got it," the man said, peeking up to his family photos on the visor overhead.

"Oh shit! The bus is slowing down!" said Buck. "Hey! That's Bling's people! Hey!" As Nitro said this Bling's aunt was helped down through the open doors of the moving bus. The woman had to fight to keep from falling as she hopped down onto the pavement.

"Fellas, I'm sorry, we gotta stop for that woman. She's in her underwear!" The rent-a-cop took charge and pulled over to pick up the woman. Buck and Nitro looked at one another, unappreciative of the choices they had before them, but knowing good and well that stopping was the right thing to do. A moment later the woman was there in the backseat with Nitro. Venting.

"I'd like to know who their mothers and fathers are!" The aunt exclaimed. "Those boys ain't got no manners what-so-ever."

"Did you see how many of them?" Buck asked.

"About four I figger'. They slingin' guns, telling everyone to take their clothes off. Somebody oughta take them boys over their knee and give'em a good lickin!"

"Jeez!" The rent-a-cop said. "There's another!" It wasn't

a moment back on the road that a 2nd passenger was let off. This time Buck could see it was the magazine reporter.

"Pass 'em," Buck told the driver.

"But he's in his *skivvies!*"

"I don't care! It's eighty-five degrees out . . . he could probably use the fresh air," Buck replied. The rent-a-cop showed guilt as he passed the waving reporter.

"Call the cops!" shouted the rent-a-cop through his opened window.

"They're still on us. I think they passed up the reporter."

"Oh. They wanna be heroes too, huh?" Elvis turned to Miles. Miles shrugged his approval. "Okay . . . you, you, you and you. Take everything off," Elvis ordered.

"Everything?" Someone asked.

"EVERYTHING!" Sonny affirmed his companion's order, unable to conceal his smile, guns at the ready. Now it was the dancer's partner, (also with the heart-shaped coochie), the rapper's uncle, and the cameraman. All of them 100% naked, stepping off the bus like they were tourists in search of a hedonism resort!

"That oughta stop 'em," said Sonny, looking back through the side view mirror. "Now make this left down the side street here," Sonny told the bus driver. "You, come in the back," he told the publicist. Sonny took another look in the mirror. The red and white Dodge had come to a stop many yards behind them. Sonny smiled broadly as though they'd already gotten away with murder. The publicist strutted towards the back of the bus, her eyes immediately searching for Bling. He was slumped there on the carpeted floor of the bus, absent of his jewels or the attitude that inevitably put him down there with that bleeding gash on his forehead. The gunmen were closing up their bags and talking amongst themselves.

"You alright, baby?" the publicist asked.

"My head. Shit. They took my shine."

She shared a look of misery with Bling, but somewhere

in her consciousness there were some of his popular lyrics
sounding off.

"GET AT ME, I'M RIGHT UP IN YOUR FACE / I'M
THE ONE WITH THE ROLEX WRIST, AND ICE THAT
BLINGS THE PLACE . . ."

CHAPTER EIGHT

"This is good . . . good. This piece alone is eighty thousand."

"Yessss," Miles exclaimed under his breath. Sasha's back office was only curtained-off, not sound proofed. It wasn't appropriate to shout and do a touchdown dance like he wanted to.

"I figure this eleven point five carats. It's good condition and its certification engraved on side here . . . see?" Sasha Franco passed an extra loupe to Miles and Miles brought it up to his eye to have a look. "The H.W. stands for Harry Winston."

Miles couldn't see what bearing that had on anything, and his face said so.

"Oh, course you wouldn't know," Sasha said, not intentionally belittling Miles but blunt just the same. "Harry Winston one of the biggest commercial jewelers on the east coast. Whoever bought this . . . maybe Fifth Avenue. Midtown." Miles looked at the crucifix wondering how a bodyguard could possess such wealth, and remembering how they'd left him laying in the back of a car. Sasha was holding a pearl necklace now. It had belonged to the rapper's mother.

"This is fabulous pearl necklace. Maybe South Seas. Twenty five, thirty thousand, easy. I maybe lose five thousand because I don't deal pearls. I must go to friend, make him a deal."

Miles said, "Whatever," knowing that $80,000 was large enough. And Sasha hadn't even begun to appraise the bulk of the catch yet.

"Now this pretty piece . . ." Miles wasn't listening anymore. He could hardly see as it was, his senses drifting out of focus, thinking about how much money he'd take away . . . how much his wedding would cost. What he'd give his mother. The numbers were building. "The Blue sapphire, ten thou. Superb Ruby Diamond ring, twenty five thou. Classic filigree diamond necklace, fifty thou. Gold ankle bracelet . . . "

Bambi was on his mind, big time. He was feeling so very accomplished right now. So successful. But would Bambi be around to celebrate? Miles would have to reach out for her. Camp out at her father's house on Rumsey Road if necessary. Go to her mother's home in Jersey and camp out if necessary. Whatever it took, Miles would do it. No matter how much money he came away with he'd never feel fulfilled unless Bambi and he made amends. Unless she'd forgive him for the little screw up the other day.

"The Rolex," mentioned Sasha, the key word waking Miles from his stupor, "is a big deal. Fourteen diamonds." Miles focused now on the yellow-gold Rolex. It had deliberately large diamond droplets about its circumference. "The diamonds alone are worth ten thou each." Miles did the calculations in his head . . . $140,000. "But when you add it up . . . wow, you really did nice this time," Sasha said, taking his attention away from the jewels and such. "Tell you what. How about I give you two hundred thou for everything."

Miles took a moment to read Sasha's eyes.

"Mr. Franco, not for nothin', but you've been good to me all these months. Really good. But see, I got friends I gotta answer to. We gotta split this up, you understand."

"I see, I see." Sasha stepped behind his desk and powered up the adding machine. The ticks and clicks sounded off in the smug office as Sasha worked out the numbers.

"Well you *did* have many small pieces as well. Tell you

what. I make it two hundred thousand today, and you can come in a few days to pick up another hundred thousand. I give you three hundred total."

"Deal." Miles had to stop himself from seeming so hasty to shake the dealer's hand. Then he waited out by the glass showcase as Sasha went into his safe to the rear of his office.

"How are you?"

"Oh, hi . . . I'm sorry Mrs. Franco. I didn't really stop to say hi. I didn't notice you."

"Oh-h-h-ho," she chuckled. "That's okay Miles. You mean well. I know. How's that girlfriend of yours?" Miles could've kicked himself for passing up on Mrs. Franco's kindness these past few visits. "She's good. Bambi's her name. And, as a matter of fact, I'm gonna make a formal proposal to her this evening." Miles told himself, *"If I can find her."*

"HOW CAN YOU afford me? Huh Miles? How can you take care of me? The things I need, my conveniences?" Bambi asked Miles this as they sat in the Sbarro's Restaurant at Times Square, way before the successful Bling heist. It was the closest and also the least expensive place he could go to considering the phony jewels he and his co-conspirators heisted from Matchstick days earlier.

But of course that was then, and this was now. Only, Miles couldn't rid himself of the memories of the things Bambi said. "You juice me up and get me all excited about going to the city . . . about a surprise, and we end up on Times Square? Sbarro's? I coulda' ordered Domino's to the house!"

Miles felt so guilty, when Bambi laid it down that day. How could he argue with her? She was 100% right. "You wanna propose to me? Offer to get me an engagement ring? Soup me up? But yet you're drivin' mommy's car, you're livin' in mommy's house, you ain't got no job, and the gas tank is on E. PLEASE Miles, tell me why you even bother to get up in the morning? How do you live with yourself? You can't even pay your own way, but you wanna pay mine." Miles was biting his lip while she read him. He lost his appetite too. "Take me home," Bambi had said to him.

* * *

It was a different story now. Miles was leaving the jeweler's shop, duffle bag full of cash in his possession, headed for a Pontiac full of expectation, all of his 3 companions likely wondering if Bling's jewelry was legitimate. He wore a confident smile because that's what he'd appreciate if *he* was on the receiving end of the cash, if *he* was one of the guys waiting in the car right now. Miles thought about making up some kind of *"I got good news and I got bad news"* effort at humor, but the guys had been through too much already. This was payday. Not all of the pay, but most of it, indeed.

"BAM!" Miles shouted once he got in the car, his voice filling the space like a loud firecracker. At the same time he snatched both straps apart so that the zipper and the duffle bag ripped open.

"OH SHIT, OH SHIT, SHIT! SHIT! SHIT!" exclaimed Sonny.

"We did it!" hollered Gus.

Elvis made two fists and pulled them in tight, a louder gesture than any other.

Miles gave each of his buddies a high five.

"How much—how much?!"

"Two hundred large. But that's not the end of it. I gotta come back in a couple days for—get this—*another* hundred. Cash. PAY DIRT!" Miles could've thrown up the bag of cash at that instant; he could've taken a small stack and tossed it out of the window to the throngs of passersby. He was that excited.

"Let's get off this block," Gus said. "I don't feel right with all these uppity cats, all the suits walkin' by-n-shit. Like I'm outta place."

The four would-be outlaws did the town. After the $200,000 was split up, each of them with pockets full of hundred dollar bills, they filled their stomachs at the Tavern On The Green restaurant in Central Park. They stopped along 11th Avenue where car dealerships ran the length of two city blocks. With fifty grand each and another twenty-five forthcoming, mostly any vehicle on the showroom floors was within their means. However, Miles made the suggestion that they merely browse and speculate, sleep on it, and come correctly a day or so later. To come with all cash was definitely not a way of coming correct, explained Miles. "Not only is that the most ghetto shit you could do, but it'll raise red flags like you wouldn't believe. Don't forget the movie about the Brink's job. *Remember*? The one with that Columbo-dude in it? Or *Goodfellas*? We gotta learn from other people's mistakes, even if other people happen to be movie actors." Miles explained that the money had to be spoon-fed into bank accounts and, when it comes time, checks should be written to the car dealerships. But in the meantime, each man picked the vehicle of his choice. Gus changed his mind, deciding against a previous selection. Now he said he wanted the black GMC Yukon, complete with 20-inch high performance chrome wheels. Sonny was heavy into the Ferrari, but it had a $150,000 price tag. So he settled for the silver Lexus GS 500, vowing to get 19inch chromes to outdo Gus. Miles said he'd buy the full-size obsidian black Mercedes S600 class, and that he'd have it bullet proofed.

After visiting a half dozen dealerships, test driving cars like they were designer shirts, they went to Columbus Avenue, to Herald Square and to the Village where they shopped for the remainder of the daylight, purchasing enough designer suits, pants and shirts. They wouldn't have to see another clothing store for at least 5 years. Gus bought enough jerseys, sweatshirts and sneakers to suit a football team. Miles went mostly for the blazers and knit pants, soft shoes and dress shirts. The casual look. He also picked up an iridescent rayon-gold 3-piece outfit fit for a Chantéuse. The tank top would drop just enough neckline to hint at Bambi's cleavage. The matching pleated pants and high collared duster would be flashy for a stage show, yet acceptable for dinner at the Rainbow Room. Miles asked if the outfit would fit the saleswoman since she was about Bambi's size. When she said yes, Miles simply told her to gift-wrap it.

When Elvis saw the dress Miles bought for Bambi he thought of Melanie, the bartender at Jimmy's. He figured her to be a size 5 and guessed that she might like something pink.

"How about this?" the saleswoman asked. "It's a hot item, suitable for a spring picnic or even a night at the movies . . ." She showed Elvis the dress on a cushioned hanger. "Would you like to see it on a model?" She asked, realizing the fellas were in the boutique to spend, not browse. A short time later a young female came out with the dress on, the saleswoman behind her. The model had to be college-going, maybe working part-time in the shop, attractive in pigtails and she was lanky according to Elvis' tastes. She did a spin and the pink, crinkled lace dress flowed in the air around her. There was a lace bodice and alternating lace / rayon georgette panels on the full skirt and sleeves. The dress had fabric-covered buttons from the v-cut (that revealed the girl's collarbone) to the waist. Elvis had to shake himself free of the mirage that stilled his senses. This wasn't Melanie in front of him.

"I want it."

"Shall I gift wrap it, like this?"

"Absolutely."

Elvis only knew Melanie from Jimmy's. He didn't get her phone number. He didn't have any idea where she lived. He only knew her name. And after a phone call, he learned her work schedule. On that Friday afternoon, just days after they received cash in hand, Elvis stopped into Jimmy's. It was early afternoon, long before the after-work crowd would spill through the doors. He immediately recognized Melanie there behind the bar wearing a bright white, slightly shaped long sleeve shirt with French cuffs. Just the first button was undone. Melanie's hair was a little different than he remembered, straighter and falling in large curls about her head. A wet look that seemed to sparkle with her movements. That brief image told Elvis he'd made the right decision. She was definitely the one. The woman he wanted. He eased up to the bar the moment she slipped out of sight, no doubt preparing for a busy night. He put his gifts down next to the high chair where he sat and deliberated over the words he'd use. He'd have to be refreshing to her. Strong but not frivolous. He'd have to play to win. Melanie glided out with a tub of ice in her hands.

"Be right with you," she said, hardly looking in Elvis' direction. It gave Elvis time to breathe at a point when he almost couldn't. Then she started to say, "What can I . . . oh. Hi there. Lemme guess . . . the Marine, right?"

"You can tell, huh?"

"Trust me soldier, I can tell. It's only been a few days. Drink?"

"Actually, I could use an orange juice. In case I choke up with what I gotta tell you."

Melanie had a quizzical look about her, pouring the orange juice, preparing a reply.

"And what would that be?" Melanie asked, her lips curling in for moisture.

Elvis took a sip, telling himself to go ahead and blurt it out.

"Melanie, yes, I remembered your name embroidered on your turtleneck last time I came here . . ."

"Okay," she smiled, appreciating that.

"I uhm . . . this is gonna sound crazy, but I gotta follow my heart, ya' know."

"O-kay. And what er' is your heart telling you?" Melanie squinted, not clear about what Elvis wanted, giving him that mock detective's gaze.

"I've been thinking about you since we talked. I mean . . . really thinking about you. Wondering what you like to do in your free time. Actually, dreaming about you."

"If this is gonna be some psycho stalker story—"

"Not at all. I'm just . . . I'm genuinely attracted to you. I just didn't know any other way to say it but to shoot from the hip. Speak my mind."

Melanie took a more concentrated position behind the bar, leaning in, elbow on the counter and chin in her palm. This seemed interesting.

"Okay. You've got my attention, as in, how'd all this happen suddenly? What're you, like, all backed up after a long tour in the Corps? *'Tour in the Corps'.* That rhymed." Elvis chuckled deep down but his smile was constant on the surface.

"Nothing like that Melanie. It's just that your face, your voice, your presence is, like, tattooed on my brain. I can't think of anything I'd like to do more than bring you joy." Melanie stared at Elvis, her mouth partially open. Brows unfurrowed.

"Could you . . . could you run that by me again?" said Melanie. Elvis swallowed. Then he reached down for the gifts. He placed them on the countertop.

"Sure, I said, your face, your voice . . ."

"No. *The part about bringing me joy.*" Melanie said this as if she couldn't believe what she'd heard. Her eyes never wavered from his.

"Right. I can't think of anything I'd like to do in the world . . . more than I'd like to bring you joy . . . pleasure and happiness. I want to wake up with the one task of . . ."

"Excuse me . . . could I have a Long Island Ice Tea please?"

"Can't you see I'm busy here?" Melanie chopped at the disruptive customer. So much for the customer always comes first.

"*Excuse me*," the man said, both angry and embarrassed.

"I brought these for you. Just a little something to let you know I'm serious," Elvis said.

Melanie put her hand to her mouth. The bouquet of flowers almost fit the width of the counter. The box next to it was large with a fat pink bow wrapped in a criss-cross. She was visibly shaken.

"A little something . . ." Melanie's voice drifted off. Now she touched Elvis' hand. "Could you wait right here?"

Melanie turned and took aggressive steps towards the end of the bar where she picked up a black purse. Elvis thought he heard her say, "You'll have to get somebody else to help you" as she disappeared past the customer through a

doorway. Elvis wondered where she was headed. The bathroom? It was just as well that she stepped away. He was
sweating like a pig under his clothes. Plus, he could get a
chance to breathe.

A loud voice sounded off from the back room. It was
distant, but Elvis and the few customers at the bar heard it.
"Whadda ya' *mean*, you quit??" Just then, Melanie emerged
from the patron's side of the bar. She approached Elvis,
picked up the flowers and the gift box. She was in a rush to
leave.

"Let's get out of here," she said.

The abrupt realization was more than what he'd expected.
Much more. But her wish was his command. Elvis looked
back over his shoulder at an angry club manager, feeling at
fault for his sudden staffing deficit, and his foots quickened
behind Melanie's.

Inside the Chevy Blazer, a plum-colored rental which
Elvis intended on driving until he decided on a car to buy,
Melanie sunk back in the passenger seat with a pensive expression. Had she just committed herself to a total stranger?
The thought was humbling, for her to have surrendered like
this. And the cabin of the Blazer somehow seemed smaller
than it actually was, where every inch of elbow room suddenly mattered. Her impulsivities catching up with her. Elvis
had no idea where he'd take Melanie, just that they should go
someplace intimate and talk. Learn more about one another.

"I live on the other side of the Major Deegan. The east
side of the Bronx," she told him. Since Elvis was headed in
that direction it was convenient to ask, "You got your own
place?"

"Mmm hmm . . . You?"

"I got a place," Elvis said.

"Maybe this is a night for sounding crazy, but I don't
know your name."

Elvis snickered as though that were the plan all along. "I
guess I never got around to that. I'm Elvis. Elvis Evans."

"No kiddin'. Your parents named you Elvis? I bet you get
a lot of jokes about your name."

"Heard 'em all. Oh Elvis, don't be cruel. Oh Elvis, Where's your blue suede shoes? Where'd you just come from Elvis? The Heartbreak hotel? Like I said, I heard 'em all." He was nonchalant about this subject as he stopped at the traffic light ready to cross North Broadway. "The worst joke was when I was younger. My schoolmates would say my parents were drinking when they named me. It bothered me back in the day but not anymore."

"So what's the truth? Why'd they name you Elvis?"

"My father tells me I was conceived in a motel out west, while he and my moms were on a cross country trip for part of their honeymoon. He told me there was a radio in their room that only tuned to one station while they were—"

"Don't tell me Elvis was on the radio when they made you."

"Exactly. But as silly as it sounds, that's what happened."

"That's not silly, that's *romantic*."

"Well at least *somebody* thinks so."

"You don't think so?"

"It is what it is. I mean, I'm fine with it 'cause I grew up with the name. It's all I've ever known. So, boom. I'm like, take it or leave it. Ya' know?"

"Sure. I'm down that way, to the left."

Elvis steered the plum-toned truck as she directed.

"So what gives Melanie? Why'd you leave the job?"

Melanie put her arm over her headrest and grabbed the bouquet from the backseat. In the rush to escape Jimmy's, she forgot about the gifts.

"I don't know Elvis," she already enjoyed saying his name. "You tell me. You always have this kind of effect on women?" Elvis said nothing, soaking in the reality of the moment. Was she committing herself to him? "I mean, our conversation was short the other day, but I sensed that you were different. I sensed that you had something special going on. I didn't care if you were Latino or black, I couldn't tell and it didn't matter. But it wasn't until today, until you said those things to me. Let's just say I'd like to get to know you better. I'd like to know if what I see is what I get."

Elvis wanted to ask if what *he* saw was what *he'd* get. But he deferred on the inquiry. He was still getting over the fact that this pretty woman was alone with him. She actually left her job to be with him. And he was still trying to make sense of it all.

CHAPTER NINE

Miles placed three unanswered calls to Bambi's Yonkers number. He reached the answering machine each time, remembering what Bambi mentioned: about her father wanting her to record the greeting. Miles was pleased at least to hear her voice. When he dialed her Jersey number Bambi's mom said she was staying with "her father." The way she'd said "*her father*" was painted with spite and venom; a tone which Miles would rather not hear again. Miles was left with mixed messages; either she was in Jersey and her mother was a good liar (acting as the gate keeper) or Bambi was indeed at her father's, not wanting to respond, still seeing Miles as a momma's boy without means.

Somewhat desperate, Miles drove to Yonkers. He was in a car the dealership loaned him, one exactly like the Mercedes he'd be purchasing, and he was intoxicated by the newness of the vehicle. That fresh start in his life. Bambi would surely realize the immediate changes: that he was accomplished now. Loaded. Miles cruised up Rumsey Road where none of the homes looked the same, but varied in their styles of middle class living, carved within a suburban environment of plentiful trees, gorgeous landscapes and a generous 2-lane asphalt street where traffic traveled at 15 and 20 miles per hour. No need to rush here.

Miles had been here before. Contemporary 2 and 3 level Tudors and Colonials. Some made of cedar, stone and red brick. Bambi's place was white stucco with columns out front. As Miles pulled into the wide driveway it struck him almost immediately that this was the first time he'd been here unannounced. There were times he dropped Bambi off. And once, when her father wasn't home, they'd had incredible sex on her bedroom floor.

For a time Miles sat there in the quiet of the luxury car, digesting the home and what it might have taken a man to obtain such a space on earth. It intimidated him to think of Bambi's father and the apparent stronghold he had on life. This was *his* house that was elevated from the street, looking down at Miles with its stacked windows, modest shrubs, the inclined lawn, a garden and wrought-iron gate.

Just before Miles had the second thought, before he put the car in reverse, he was startled at the sight of another vehicle easing into the driveway next to him. Not as concerned with the make of the car, a Mercedes comparable to his, Miles swallowed at his Adam's apple, knowing in his heart who this was. The car motor died and the older man seemed to collect his things while clearly curious about the stranger before exiting his car. Miles felt behooved to get out and introduce himself. He had flowers and gifts in the back of the car, but left them alone for the time being.

"How are you sir, I'm Miles." Miles reached out to shake his hand, and took notice of the slender build, business attire and experienced eyes. "*A friend of Bambi's.*" Her father's eyes appraised Miles and then the car. Miles didn't want to seem the least bit disingenuous. He kept sincere eye contact and he kept it humble.

"Okay," He answered, inviting further comment.

"Well, Mr. Miller to be totally honest, I've been wanting to meet you."

"Is that so."

"Yes sir. I'm in love with your daughter. I want to marry her."

"Is *that* so?" Mr. Miller said with a discerning gaze. "You'd better come in then."

* * *

Miles dared not say a word at this point, nothing like, *"Wow, nice place you got here,"* or *"I've never seen a ceiling this high."* Better that Miles just keep his mouth shut. What was that wise quote that Miles recalled? *"Better to not say a word and be a fool than to open your mouth and remove all doubt."* Miles was too high when he'd first come through these doors, onto these finished hardwood floors and under the 30 ft vaulted ceilings. He had been high with passion and filled with lust. Too excited to have paid any mind to Mr. Miller's standard of living. But now that he got a better look he was still far from relaxed, and sex was the furthest from his mind.

"Can I get you something to drink?" Miles wondered if it was a trick question. If he said no would that seem too obvious an answer? Or would he seem like a nerd who wasn't with the in crowd? And if he said yes, would it mean irresponsibility since he was driving? Or would it say that there were other such mind-altering stimulants in his routine? It was a no-win position to be placed in.

"Well, you know I'm driving, but I don't want to seem unappreciative."

"How 'bout some apple cider."

"I wouldn't mind that at all sir." Miles admired the 3-sided fireplace and some of the Afro-centric art hanging before accent lighting. There was a sculpture of a couple slow dancing and another perhaps the same couple, hot footing, positioned at opposite sides of the room. There were tall book cases set in the walls and modern lighting throughout the open areas. And Miles could see an absence of plants, feeling that Mr. Miller might be missing that woman's touch.

"So tell me, Miles. Where you from?"

"Here in Yonkers. Over on Warburton."

"Oh."

"I went to school at Roosevelt. Did two years in college. The Westchester Business Institute."

"Heard of it. So you're planning on your own business?"

"I might be partnering up with a friend to open up a clothing store at the Galleria in White Plains."

"Oh. Enterprising, are we. Tell me how a young buck like you goes from the hood to owning your own store."

"Part owner."

"Of course."

"Little odd jobs. Saving up. Stuff like that."

"And you can afford to buy yourself a Mercedes?"

Miles felt like his story might fall apart if he wasn't careful. Mr. Miller was sharp as a tack.

"Well, the Mercedes is a loaner from the dealer. I'm planning on leasing one like it, and . . . I guess he's trying to close the sale." The calculations even sounded correct Miles, surprising himself with his quick thinking. "My buddy is getting some money to start up the business, so, ya' know. I'm gonna have to start lookin' professional. Stop depending on mom."

"What's your mom's name?"

"Theresa."

"And are your parents together?"

"Afraid not. I never knew my father."

"Mmm . . . sorry to hear that."

"It's cool. It's like, what you don't know won't hurt you."

"Never looked at it that way." Mr. Miller sipped from his own glass of cider. "So, care to tell me what's up with Bambi?"

"It feels funny speaking to you—her father—about this, but *I do* really love her. And that's not just a word I'm using. I feel warm inside when I hear her voice, even when I say her name or think about her. She has a special energy that feeds me. Makes me wanna go out and take on the world."

"And that's why you want to marry her."

"Not only. It's not about what she can do for me. It's not. I feel as though I've been put here to make her happy. To protect her. To pamper her. I haven't stopped thinking about Bambi since the day we met. And I don't think that'll ever change. Did you ever meet someone and think that your life just wouldn't be complete without them?"

"Hmmm . . ." Miller chortled and said, "Bambi's mother."

Miles sensed the salt in the elder man's tone. He also

remembered the spite and venom that the Mrs. stressed when he called. Maybe love wasn't such a good subject after all. "But that's us. I'd be silly to see you and my daughter as I see myself and Bambi's mother. So I'll just say this. Hopefully, or eventually—that is if it's in Bambi's wishes to agree on marriage—you and I can get to know each other better. Something that certainly doesn't take a day or an hour to do. However, I want to be clear about this; that's my daughter we're talking about. I'm her protector before you are. If you should fall by the wayside, she'd likely be coming to her father if there's something she can't handle . . . if there's something she needs a man for. I will not tolerate any physical abuse what-so-ever. You will never raise a hand to my daughter. And you will respect my daughter as you would your mother. And I certainly hope you've got home training and that you respect your mother."

"Oh yes, sir. If I may say, I can't imagine anyone putting an abusive hand on Bambi, much less myself. It'll never happen."

"Refill?"

Miles shook his head no and asked, "Any idea where Bambi is?"

"She's usually here when I get home. You're welcome to wait." Mr. Miller's words stilled mid-syllable upon hearing keys and laughter at the front door.

"Daddy! Daddy!"

"In here snookums."

Miles wondered what was humorous, and if she was alone or not.

"Daddy, I have a friend—" Bambi emerged from the front entry of the house and realized the surprise. A man of 6 ft with a crew cut, an oversized blue sweat suit, and fresh-out-of-the-box white Nikes was a foot or so behind her. Miles' senses fogged up. "Oh. I see we have company," Bambi said.

Mr. Miller held back from making the face he had in store: a face that might've questioned his daughter's choices in men. She had a white boy in his house. *Oh, brother.*

Miles came to life, prompted by Mr. Miller's pat on his shoulder.

"Okay well, I just got in and I haven't had a chance to unwind, so I'm gonna let you young folks mix amongst yourselves."

Miles heard Mr. Miller excusing himself and felt the encouraging squeeze on his arm. But Miles somehow wanted to disappear, too. Who was this dude? And what did he have goin' on that Miles didn't?"

Bambi trotted over to her dad, pulling at his elbow once their conversation was far enough away.

"Daddy, aren't you gonna help me?" Bambi with the low voice.

"Baby doll, you're a grown woman. You've got your own choices to make in life. But can I ask what possesses you to want to be with a white boy?"

"Daddy, he's just a friend. *God.* This isn't the segregated sixties. Ease up."

"Hmmm . . ." Her father touched her cheek. "I just want what's best for you. Don't mind me." He started off again, but turned back to Bambi and said, "But I *do* like Miles." And they shared a look before he went on his way.

Miles wasted no time, already sneaking a peek at Bambi's friend, sizing him up, wondering if he'd twisted her out on the bedroom floor, too. But there was that look about him that told Miles different. This kid didn't have a chance over him. Miles was cool. Miles had it together finally. And, as if the spirits in the midst had convincing evidence, Miles always had Bambi screaming, crying or moaning with pleasure. These thoughts pushed Miles to approach Bambi for a one-on-one.

"Bambi what gives. I've been calling and calling. I've been having some difficulties, but all that's changed now."

Miles wasn't just saying the right words. He was beckoning. Practically begging, but with some pride in his manner. She originally had her hand on her hip, but then she folded her arms, wanting to hear this. Wanting to hear more. Bambi knew Miles didn't have any idea who her friend was, but it was thrilling to see and hear him face up to the challenge and to lay it on the line like he did.

"I'm moving out from Mom's this week. I'm getting a new car." Bambi had wondered about the 2nd Mercedes in the driveway. "I even got you this . . ."

Miles took out a small velvet gift box and held it out with two hands as he opened it. Bambi's mouth opened and she took in as much air as her body could stand. In the meantime, Miles went down on one knee, ignoring that there was an onlooker, a possible suitor of Bambi's. But he could care less. This was his one moment in time. His heartbeat banged in his chest.

"Bambi you mean the world to me. There could never be another you. I go to sleep with you every night and wake up with you every morning. You're the only woman on my mind. I can't even think straight when you're away. I . . ." Bambi lost her composure. Her anger turned to compassion, and her will power turned to mush. She was breathing heavily, shivering even, and she couldn't stand it anymore.

Miles thought he'd die there on his knees when Bambi turned away and strutted toward the other man in the room. But then he overheard her words.

"Rick, listen, you gotta go. I'll call you later. Come on." And just like that, Bambie escorted this Rick-fella to the front door and shut it behind him. Rick hadn't said a word either way.

CHAPTER TEN

When Melanie said she'd be a few minutes, Elvis had no idea where she was going or what she was doing. He simply made himself at home like she said. He was amused by her cute studio, the basement of a two family house which had been converted and finished. She had a futon set, including a couch, a papasan and a queen-size bed that lay barren on the carpeted floor. Next to the bed was a clock-radio and a cordless phone. There was a fish tank and a parakeet. And there were enough house plants to create an illusion that this was an indoor garden, not the residence of a single woman.

It was when Melanie came from another room in a black satin kimono that Elvis had to rub his eyes. Was she for real? At first sight, she might've been naked underneath. Elvis saw nothing but the kimono and her bare skin. Melanie's legs could've belonged to a figure skater, her pinned-back hair to a raven and her curves to a sculpture. It was hard to believe this was *her*. But then Melanie reached for a light switch and the lights dimmed. She stood in the center of the room, in front of the papasan where Elvis sat, and she pulled the kimono apart like curtains.

"You like?"

Elvis wondered if he should praise God now or later as Melanie stood there in her black bra and panties, virtually offering him kingdom come. His throat went dry and his rectum constricted unconsciously as he stuttered his reply.

Melanie approached Elvis and she took his head in her hands, toying with his ears. Then she bent down to kiss him on the lips. A sweet kiss that was trite, yet assuring. She stood erect again and softly pulled his baby face into her fragrant cleavage. Elvis nuzzled there like a happy infant, ready for whatever she had in store, but nervous just the same. If this was the reward for his recent success, then he was ready to accept it with total abandon. With his hands smoothing along her calves, her thighs and her ass, Elvis felt electricity from her skin, her fine peach fuzz playing against his finger tips like a live current. Eventually he unclasped the brassiere and freed her breasts. She took the clothing and draped it over his head as he nuzzled his face once again, this time working himself up to tender kisses and gentle nibbles. He took her nipples in his mouth and made his tongue glide around them, making them wet and hard. As he did this Melanie gasped and moaned in concert with his actions, clutching his face and scalp all the while, wanting him and owning him simultaneously.

For Melanie, this had been a long awaited dream come true. It was this recurring fantasy where the man of her dreams would approach the bar at Jimmy's and he'd say all the right things. He'd be cute, but leave so much more to her imagination. There was an instant back at the café when *Elvis was* that *man*. She'd snapped, knowing that this would be the evening when she'd give it all or nothing. After all, she figured, you only live once.

And now this man who would otherwise be a perfect stranger was not just *offering* to shower her with flowers and gifts, but he was *doing it. He overwhelmed her.* And those words . . . they were stapled to her mind now: *I can't think of anything I'd like to do more than bring you joy.* Wow. There had been guys who wanted nothing more than to show her the night of her life . . . or the weekend of her life . . . And for the most part, pieces of those promises came true. Except, the decisions she made . . . the men to whom she said yes were always previously committed, or worse, married. They never told the truth. They always had skeletons. It had depressed her. Sent her to using stimulants to lift her up when she was down. And, quiet as it was kept, she was still hooked to those dependencies. Drinking was her haven when she needed it. Smoking weed was her crutch. And when she needed total refuge, she mixed china white with the weed.

But now, finally, here was Elvis. He could be her security blanket. And if she was lucky, maybe he'd turn out to be everything else she needed. At worst, she'd at least feel the full force of his pleasure. She'd be receptive to his energy and power. She'd enjoy his thrusting and pounding as much as he'd enjoy giving it to her.

He had her fully undressed now, and she was teeming with anxiety, wanting to be naked against his naked body. She switched places with Elvis, prompting him to stand, then she undressed him. She unbuttoned his shirt and stripped him of his tee, leaving the clothing at his feet. Then Melanie sat before him, looking up with submissive intent, and she unbuckled his pants, pulling them and the boxer shorts down over his engorged muscle. There were some women who saw this as a "no-no". On that scale, Melanie saw this as a "never." But right now there was no question about what she'd do. She wanted Elvis in every way and in all ways. She wanted to show him just exactly what she had to offer him; and fuck leaving something for later. The hell with rainy days. There could be times for experimenting. As for now, Melanie rented experiences from the past to (if possible) send this particular man to the moon and back, right into her waiting arms.

Moments lingered as Melanie taunted Elvis, her hand firmly gripping him as she kissed here and there, enjoying the throbbing pulse that pushed at her palm and even his fingers combing through her disheveled hair. But she didn't intend on him waiting long or for him to agonize with desire. No. Melanie took him in her mouth entirely. She hugged him with her frenzied tongue. With her eyes shut she imagined that this was Heaven for Elvis, her succulent sounds mixing with his hearty, grunting proclamations, creating a give-and-take melody that went from affection to compulsion.

Melanie wanted to go further. To change positions so that they might feed one another. But Elvis exploded with a loud growl. His hands both unrelenting; overpowering her, with his fingers weaved into knots about her hair, holding her captive to receive his ejaculate. The realization of a possible end made her misty eyed as Elvis sat spent there between her lips. Her breathing had been stifled and she gagged slightly, but it was something she'd handled in the past. She'd handle it now.

Elvis wanted to collapse onto Melanie's bed. His legs had long since buckled and his mind was traveling in circles that made dizzy seem normal. But there were feelings and emotions here. A puzzle that had to be worked out. Some understanding.

The two eventually braided themselves in each other's arms, lost in speechless wonder, reflecting on what was and hoping for what might be. Elvis didn't want to speak. He didn't want to mess up something that was potentially his final frontier—the woman of his dreams. At the same time, Melanie was both ashamed and nervous.

Sure, she'd given him something that he wanted . . . or at least something his body wanted. But at what cost? Would this be a one night stand? She didn't want that. She didn't need that. She needed him. But for the time being, maybe there would be answers when they woke. Elvis dozed off. And so Melanie went there with him, her cheek to his bare chest and her hands wandering until they too ran out of gas.

CHAPTER ELEVEN

Sasha Franco never reached out to Miles. There was no need to. Miles did what he did, and then he brought his catch to 47th Street where the jeweler's business was established. So when Miles' pager went off, he was surprised to see Sasha's phone number, a number that had become more and more familiar to Miles with each passing venture.

"Who was that?" Bambi asked as she adjusted her bra and turned her back to Miles so that he could hook the clasp on the straps. They had just finished another wild session, this time at a room up in the Marriot hotel on Times Square. It was another show of how Miles would no longer be penny-pinching. Evidence that he could afford skip-the-limit expenditures.

"Ah, the jeweler, actually." Miles wondered if he should share such confidential details; how Sasha was virtually a part of his crimes and all. But then again, he did bring Bambi there. And Bambi did meet Mrs. Franco. Then, of course, there was the ring. "I made arrangements to drop by to pay the balance on the engagement ring," said Miles with the perfect excuse.

Bambi smiled. She still had the ring on. Wouldn't take it off, even during the sex. Miles winced at the thought of the ring, it having scratched his thigh when she mounted him.

"It's such a beautiful ring, Miles. I love you so much, I'm gonna be a wonderful wife to you."

"I don't have a doubt in the world about that, boo." Miles was so spent right now, so immersed in this pillow-talk. But he was busy too, throwing on clothes so that he could get to Sasha. There was the balance of the money. $100,000. Plus, Sasha said he had a "proposition."

His pockets were full again. No need to go through any arduous counting, either. Miles was more than certain all of the money was there. But Sasha was anxious, more than he was when Miles first stopped by with Bling's prize catch.

"So what gives? What's this proposition you wanted to discuss?" Miles said this, partially relieved that the said proposition wasn't some interruption of the $100,000 balance.

"Have a seat, Miles." Sasha pulled his chair around from his desk so that the two would see eye-to-eye with no encumbrances between them. Sasha explained to Miles that there was this group of jewelers on 47th that formed The Diamond Club. In politics, the equivalent might be the Presidential advisors. In boxing, it would be the Commission. In a Fortune 500 company, it would be the board of directors. But like the President's decisions are guided by the advisors, as the Commission oversees the rules and direction of boxing, and as the CEO's of the world control the ways and means of how companies are run, so too does The Diamond Club regulate the processes and prices of diamond transactions of that dynasty; that very strip along 47th street.

The Diamond Club is an elite group. Any ole diamond dealer can't become a member. You must fit a certain unknown criteria. You must have certain connections. It was all about who you knew. Sasha Franco was not a part of The Diamond Club. He saw the group and its monopoly over the majority's trading practices as Communism at its best.

"I receive information this week. Confidential information. It is the African Queen Emerald. It is forty carats. The finest, largest cut emerald in North America. She is exquisite, perfection, a brilliant fire. Impeccable with hearts and arrows." Miles was lost in Sasha's accolades for a time, wondering if he'd ever come around to the point. Sasha was saying stuff about De Beers, The Syndicate and the American Gem Society, but Miles let it go in one ear and out of the other. "Diamond is worth millions. And it's here in the United States." Sasha was excited by his own energy, pumping himself up with each word. "I'm thinking we can make a deal." Finally, he had Miles's attention.

This was called an emergency meeting, meaning that Gus would have to pull away from the wax job he was applying (the 2nd in just as many days) to his new GMC Yukon; Sonny would have to set aside his footwork he was doing to gather details about the Galleria project and the clothing store he wanted to open there; and Elvis would need to set aside any gun sales for the day. Miles explained that this was a confidential meet; that meant just the four of them.

For the occasion, Miles reserved a table in the furthest section of Mr. Leo's, the soul food cuisine in lower Manhattan. By one in the afternoon, the scheduled time, the former Marine Corps recruits were sitting around a table far away from possible exposure of their conversation. Meanwhile, Miles was explaining details of the proposal.

"I'll be the first to say that it sounds sweet, Miles. I just wonder how anyone can move around with million-dollar diamonds like this. No Brink's truck? No armed escorts? And the guy doesn't pack a gun? Doesn't this sound just a little nuts to you?"

"Maybe it is nuts, Elvis. But my information is rock solid. I'd bet my life on it."

"So," Sonny jumped in. "We're supposed to follow some mangy Jewish dude with thick glasses and scraggly hair."

"Scraggly *black* hair."

"Right. And this guy is supposed to be a doofus. Supposed to be stupid as a lump of clay. Carrying around a stone. How many carats did you say?"

"Forty."

Sonny shook his head in disbelief. Then said, "Listen, whatever. I'm in. Just lemme know my part. But I'm packin' heavy for this. Ain't no way I'm lettin' down my guard 'cause shit is supposed to be sweet."

"I'm with you all the way, dog. We win this, I retire. Me and Melanie are gonna do Never Never Land at Michael Jackson's ranch."

"Shit, you? I'mma open a car wash in the BX. I'm startin' to like this whole truck waxin' bit. I can't go robbin' jewels all my life, right?" Gus said. "Plus I can put some money up for a lawyer to help with my father's appeal."

"What's the breakdown Mile's?" asked Sonny. The table hushed as the waitress brought over the food. When she left, Miles said, "Two hundred and fifty thousand each."

Gus choked on the salad he'd just forked into his mouth. He sounded convincing enough that Sonny was patting his back, telling him to *drink some water.*

Taking Gus's outburst as nothing serious, Elvis asked, "When did you plan on doing the lick?"

"In ten days," said Miles. "We're gonna need four car rentals, 2-way radios with a dedicated frequency, and we're gonna have to figure out alternative plans. Like we did with the naked bodies on the bus."

"You mean, we might have to put some more nudes out on the street?" Gus said this while laughing.

"Not quite Gus. We just need a back up plan . . . gotta be prepared for whatever."

"For a quarter of a million? I'll do all the preparing you want," said Elvis.

They left Mr. Leo's with stars in their eyes. All of them with their heads fucked up. A quarter of a million dollars. Money that they otherwise would never possess in this lifetime, or at least never planned it that way. Miles simply affirmed what he already knew: that his partners in crime would go with the project. But Gus and Sonny were numb with gratuitous imaginings. All Gus could see was a fleet of GMC trucks and a big home with room enough to park them. Sonny thought about expanding on his Galleria project. He wondered if he'd have enough to buy the mall, to set up more than one clothing store to make it look like they were competing. All the other big clothing chains seemed to be doing it. Elvis wanted to give up the gun business and all the riff raff that came with it. It seemed like he was a magnet for every dope dealer, gang member and ruffian in the South Bronx. All of them with their con games, conspiracies and underground ethics. In some way, considering what he and the others were involved with, Elvis could assimilate with these figures. But in the depths of his soul he knew that selling guns in the hood wasn't his scene. All the risks and dangers that came with the trade was not his way of life. Now that the finances looked promising, he could care less about the meager markup or the profit he'd make on a nine millimeter, a Glock or a .38 special. With the $50,000 he got from the Bling lick, plans were already in motion for him and Melanie to move into Manhattan. In fact, a real estate broker was scouting for a place now. He expected to get rid of the Chevy Blazer as soon as he had a chance to visit the dealership, but Melanie was keeping him occupied. She didn't want him to leave her sight, and even when he wanted to leave, he couldn't. The two fucked, ordered fast food, fucked, rented movies, fucked, smoked weed, fucked, bathed in champagne, then fucked some more. They were part of a cycle that was perfectly fine with them and nobody else's business. Elvis and Melanie went out to dinner on occasion, they took in a movie and drove up to Playland, the amusement park up in Rye, New York. They stopped by The Wedge to tip the topless dancers. And *always* when they got back home, they got high and fucked some more. Miles, on the other hand, had so much more on his mind than the others. The African Queen heist was the beginning of married life. It was his destiny with Bambi and the children they'd make. He'd be able to retire early, drawing a small salary as the absentee owner of the Galleria project. Sonny would run it all, while Miles would get his checks in the mail. Simple. In the meantime, he intended on traveling, showing off his new wife to the world. He'd also invest in her singing career and see to it that her dreams were achieved. Whatever she

wanted, he'd buy. A dress? Done. A car? Done. Another child?
Two or three? Done. Done. Done. He'd search for property
in what *Black Enterprise Magazine* rated as the best African
American cities. He'd consider Houston, Texas or Atlanta,
Georgia but he'd lean towards Charlotte, North Carolina
because there was less crime to beware of. He'd have children to think about. Miles seemed to have it all mapped out.
Just like anything else, with proper planning his dream
would also become reality.

The lick was set for Monday morning. But for the previous
two weeks, Elvis, Sonny, Miles and Gus took turns and
partnered up to follow Matthew Kats, the jewelry salesman
who was in possession of the African Queen diamond. If
they weren't following Matthew, they were completing a
checklist of tasks to successfully carry out the hit. Matthew
lived in Hartsdale, New York, not far from where Sonny
lived in White Plains. His colonial home was around the
corner from the Wingfoot Country Club & Golf Course,
in a community that was a step above suburban and just
short of gated. The man drove a Volkswagen Bug that was
deep ocean blue. He generally left home at 7am, pulled
into the Stop-n-Go for a Pepsi and a couple of the newspapers that weren't already delivered to the house. Then it
was on to the Exxon station for gas before he finally took
the Cross Westchester Expressway to the N.Y. State Through-
way, to East River Drive. The expressways took Matthew
straight to 42nd street where he drove a few blocks to a
parking garage right in the hub of the 47th street's diamond
exchange.

On 47th street, Matthew was seen empty handed as he entered GENUINE JEWELERS, the company he worked for.
Within an hour he'd leave the building with an attaché case
handcuffed to his wrist. To see this was exciting. It meant that,
unequivocally, this feeble little fellow was carrying something
of great value. Something that, with the help of a pair of steel
handcuffs, was affixed to his very own mortality.

From GENUINE JEWELERS, Matthew went back to

the garage and drove his beetle away from the diamond district. Sasha Franco had warned Miles that 47th street had plainclothes police as well as rent-a-cop services, which watched over that strip where jewelers operated shops between Broadway and Avenue of the Americas. Beyond that, he said, was open season.

Matthew made various stops to jewelry stores in Manhattan, including a couple of department stores. From the city, he drove out to Long Island on Mondays, to New Jersey on Tuesdays, to Westchester on Wednesdays, to Connecticut on Thursdays, and on Fridays he'd remain in-house at GENUINE JEWELERS or he'd visit some of the other jewelers on 47th, hold his own office meetings, etcetera. At 4pm on Fridays the Diamond Club convened. Always, Matthew headed home to Hartsdale for a quiet 6 o'clock dinner with his wife. And always, the attaché case was locked up back at the office. "So why don't we just hit this dude when he goes out to Westchester or Connecticut? Why we waitin' for a specific Monday?" asked Gus when he and Miles did the Wednesday and Thursday tailing.

"Because he's carrying light. Only a few hundred thousand. Our inside man says Monday is the day."

"Only a few hundred? This could've been easier than the Bling lick."

"What, and miss out on the music video? The dancers with the pubic hearts?" Miles provoked a laugh from Gus. "But seriously, as I understand it, this will be a one shot deal. The guy's never been hit before, so he's set in his ways. He's into a routine that he thinks is un-fuck-wit'-able. That's probably why he's okay with carryin' the big dog, the African Queen."

"You still haven't told us how this is goin' down. What're the rental cars for?"

"Everything in its right time, Gus."

"And what about the security escorts that see him to and from his car? What're we gonna' knock them off like we did the queer-bodyguard?"

"Not even close. I'm tellin' you, Gus, we're gonna' discuss

this over the weekend. Relax and trust me. We've done good so far, haven't we?"

Gus shrugged in agreement, thinking he was probably being over anxious.

The conspirators got together for a final sit-down on the African Queen job. For weeks Miles had held back on how they'd execute this, wanting to preserve the integrity of the effort. There was one other concern that Miles needed to address.

"Okay, okay, let's get serious here. Time to get down to business." Miles said this as the four sat eye-to-eye in the dining room of Well's, an establishment which managed to maintain its popularity amongst Harlem's best soul food restaurants. "Two important questions here. Anybody having second thoughts?" The four traded glances, but said nothing or else shrugged off the idea. "Okay then, Sonny did you take care of the vehicles."

"It's done. We got two rent-a-wrecks, both of 'em can handle a day's work. At least. And I got two picks-ups. I had to do some shady shit to get 'em with a phony name-n-all, but it's done. The wheels are all waiting in the municipal garage on one twenty fifth street."

"Why one twenty fifth?"

"It's central to us all. Plus it's one of the only spots that I can trust. I paid a crack head five dollars to watch them day and night."

"Good work Sonny. Elvis, what's up on the two-ways?"

"I should have 'em tomorrow. They're—"

"They got exclusive frequency?"

"That's what I was about to say. The dude I know, the hacker, he's gonna have that done by tomorrow."

"You sure?"

"Double sure."

"Well, I guess it's about time we get right down to it." Miles unfolded a diagram, the sheet of paper almost filling the whole table. "This is the road map I drew of our friend's routine. Here's the Queens-Midtown Tunnel, the Long Island Expressway, and Holbrook, where he's going to pick up the diamond. He'll be going to an office building that's isolated *right* . . . here. Now we all know a little bit about Long Island, 'cause we just pulled off a job there. But this is another story, entirely. I don't want to get caught up with some local cop who we'll have to take out for getting in our way. Now, I've already taken the drive out to Holbrook, a place called Harry Winston . . ."

"Who's Harry Winston?" asked Elvis.

"It's not a who. That's the name of the company. Their office building is wide open. No gates or fences. Just a lawn, trees and a parking lot where a rent-a-cop drives around every now and then."

"So we're gonna hit 'em right there?"

"No. We want him to leave without a hitch. We want him to get away from any local cops who might wanna play hero. Let 'em get onto the parkway." Miles traced the route he expected Matthew to take to the Long Island Expressway. "Once he hits the expressway? He's ours. We know where the highway patrol sits . . . here. . . . and here. The key is to make our move between Central Islip and . . . Deer Park. There's a twenty minute window between these two exits. And if our inside man is correct, the salesman will be on the L.I.E., Monday afternoon, with the African Queen."

"I got you," Sonny smiled, reading between the lines before anyone else. "We're gonna run him off the *road*. Fucking *brilliant*."

"Exactly, Sonny. We're gonna stay in touch by 2-way, block him off from three sides, run him off. There's a grassy ditch right about here, just after the Central Islip exit. We snatch the attaché . . ." Miles was holding a handcuff key so that it dangled like some hypnotist's pendant. "And if this doesn't work I've got bolt cutters. If they don't work, I'll have a chainsaw in the trunk of the car as a last resort."

"Chainsaw? The handcuffs ain't made out of no wood. That shit is steel or something."

"You're right, Gus. But his wrist is made out of skin and bone."

"Oh *shit*," exclaimed Gus, the air pushing out with his words.

"But, of course, that's only a last resort."

CHAPTER TWELVE

Elvis had his eyes closed. Squeezed so tight that his forehead had a slight throb off pain, the blood rushing around his brain in a small whirlpool. But this was a good pain. Melanie was there on her futon bed with him, naked, splayed and scooted down with her head at his groin. She was giving him major attention again. Licking at him as she would an almond ice cream pop. When she got him wet enough to glisten, Melanie reached into some tinfoil near the bed and took up a pinch of cocaine. Then she sprinkled it over Elvis's swollen penis and positioned herself to straddle him so that she could take him little by little. The cocaine caused his penis to vibrate with excitement, a phenomena that made Melanie crazy with spasm after spasm, until the climaxes were self perpetuating, acting alone.

Just as Elvis was about to succumb, before he could consciously let go of that intense accumulation deep down in his loins, Melanie's accumulation deep down in his loins, Melanie's front door imploded. The interruption was so shocking an act that Elvis exploded anyway, ejaculating onto Melanie's pelvis as he pulled out of her. It was a strange experience for him, to be satisfied and scared to death all at once.

"Put some clothes on," said the intruder to both lovers. His voice was calm but in charge.

"Rose! But . . . what . . ." Elvis was trying to find the right words in his embarrassment. Meanwhile he held a pillow over his dripping penis as he scrambled for clothes. Melanie seem disoriented, reaching for things that weren't there, her eyes only halfway visible under lowered lids.

"What's up with her?" Misa said to Liza, both of Rose's women companions armed and suited to kill, looking at Melanie like some unfolding horror.

"That's him. He's one-a–dem," said a fourth voice coming through the broken door once it was safe to do so. Elvis apparently tried to make sense of things as if his mind wasn't confused with images, thoughts and sounds. When he realized who just walked over the threshold he said, "*OH SHIT*", under his breath, knowing damn well that he was ass-deep in trouble. Bling was wearing darker clothing than Elvis might've remembered. Darker than the bright whites and reds he was wearing weeks ago on his tour bus. At the same time, Melanie had a blanket held to her chest, but it was a wasted effort with both her nipples still exposed. Liza holstered the pistol she had under her arm and bent down to pick up the foil beside the bed. She approached Rose with it. He took it, dabbed his pinkie in the anthill of coke and touched it to his tongue. A second later he spit and wiped the back of his arm against his lips. All this while still holding two loaded Ruger pistols.

"I don't know what I ever saw in you, dude," Rose said. Elvis stood there with a sheepish, sleepy look about him.

Bling had a build-up of rage inside of him. "Mothafucka, I wanna beat the shit out of him."

"Bling!" As Rose called his name, Misa put her arm out to stop the rapper in his steps. Not that she (or Liza) were any kind of muscled-up goons, but the respect they maintained as Rose's girls was powerful in itself. Not to mention the guns they toted. "I didn't finance your career for you to be a thug. I put you in business to pretend. Now pretend to disappear. We'll take care of this." Rose made a face that likely carried a lifetime's worth of wrath. Bling turned to jelly, his shoulders in a slump and his face spiritless. Seconds later, like magic, he disappeared from Melanie's studio.

Rose called Misa by head-nod alone.

"Take her in the hallway." Misa did, leaving Liza to cover Rose's back as he addressed Elvis. From inside the residence Misa's voice could be heard clearly. "SIT!"

"Okay buddy. We got us a little problem here that I know you'll help me with because I know that you value your life. There was a certain robbery that took place a few weeks ago. A certain rapper and his family and friends were stripped and their valuables were ripped off." Rose lifted his hand to quiet Elvis before he said a word. "Naw nigga, don't say **SHIT** until I finish with what I gotta say." And Elvis deflated back into his stupor. "Now, the problem is not so much that there was a robbery, 'cause I'm not the police. And Lord knows how I make my living from selling guns to robbers, burglars and thieves. But, see . . . this has become sort of personal because *that* rapper? That rapper is an investment of mine. Whoever took from him? Took from me. So now that robbery . . . those jewels (watches, rings, bracelets-n-shit) were really my loss. And I don't take losses, I create them. The last person to try a move on me was left layin' in a social club up on White Plains Road.

"So here's what I'm gonna ask you. And since you know me personally, I'll trust you to tell me the truth because, again, I know you value your life. Now . . ." Rose pulled up a chair and he sat down ready to hear a testimony. "You know something about this, don't you?"

Elvis had been sitting there on the bed, dumbfounded. But somehow Rose's questions pierced the state of dementia that Elvis was going through, and Elvis nodded in reply to Rose's question.

Rose said, "Good. I think we're gonna work this out just fine. Maybe I'll even let you live after this. Maybe. Now that we're on a roll I want you to tell me where the goods are, including the money." Rose had a face of stone, fully intending on achieving his objective.

"We—we—" Elvis coughed, perhaps choking on the words he tried to get out of his mouth. "We sold it all."

"We sold it all." Rose nodded, grimaced and turned to his girl Liza. When he turned back to face Elvis with his sweaty brow, temples and upper lip, Rose asked, "Who in the fuck is we?"

"The crew I run with."

"The crew. And does this crew have a name? Who's running this thing?"

"No name. Just Gus and Sonny and Miles-n-me. Miles really calls all the shots."

"Oh really."

"Yeah. We all just follow his orders," said Elvis, trying hard to remove the blame from his shoulders. "Plus, I really just started runnin' with them. I only did one hit with 'em."

"And this Miles dude, he has the money you got for the shit you stole?"

"Well . . ." Elvis scratched his head. "Not exactly . . . We kinda split the money up between the four of us."

"You, Miles, Gus and Sonny," said Rose, wanting to print those names firmly on the wall of his mind.

"Yes."

"And I suppose you gonna tell me you spent all your money."

Elvis lowered his head. Shame. "I got a little left," he said.

"Your cut was how much?"

"About fifty," Elvis lied.

"So . . ." Rose calculated the numbers in his head. "You all sold the shit for two hundred gees."

"Somethin' like that, yeah."

"And you spent fifty grand in three weeks."

"Uh . . ." Elvis hardly got a word out before Rose reached out and bitch-slapped him across the face.

"Now. I'll ask you again. You spent fifty grand in three weeks."

Elvis had been knocked back on the bed and was still holding his cheek, wondering what hit him.

"I put a down payment on a penthouse. I put a down payment on a ride. I bought a kilo of coke."

"A kilo? A fuckin' kilo?"

Rose was reminded of his late cousin Tucker who originally worked under Freeze, (the kingpin from the BX), until he crossed the guy and began buying coke from Sosa. Rose remembered how Tucker would then buy his stuff for 25 grand per kilo . . . before Freeze had him killed.

"Goddamn crack head . . . I should," Rose pulled back to swing again. But Elvis cried out and cringed at the same time.

"Wait—wait—wait we got more . . . more! We're gettin' more tomorrow!"

Rose froze in motion. "More?"

"Yeah, more. We're doin' a big hit tomorrow. Worth millions."

"You full-a-shit."

"No. I'm tellin' you the truth. We're hittin' this Jewish dude. A lame. He's supposed to be carryin' the African Queen tomorrow. Over forty carats. *The real thing.*"

Rose thought about this, then he said, "And you and your crew are supposed to do this tomorrow."

"All planned out."

"Tell me more."

On Sunday evening Miles and Bambi went for a drive in his brand new S Class Mercedes 600. It was just as he ordered, obsidian black, and it glistened like a proud black diamond. He took her up the Bronx River Parkway, down the Hutchinson River Parkway, and along the Cross-Bronx Expressway until they parked under the George Washington Bridge and necked like silly teenagers. As if the water wasn't murky and polluted by day, the night lights that stood out along the New Jersey side of the bridge reflected off of the Hudson River as well as the hood of the car. It was all so stimulating! And the summer's breeze was giving way to fall's chill, a sort of indecisive period for Mother Nature.

Miles submerged himself in these kisses, fondling Bambi and touching her as though she was still virgin. Something in his experience told Miles that these moments wouldn't be the same further along in their relationship. The newness of it all would be missing and they might even take affection for granted. And although Miles sensed this, he didn't speak on it, busy answering the call of his mind's pleasure center, a doorway that had been jammed open over these past weeks as Bambi continued to feed Miles more and more of herself.

If breathing freely wasn't necessary they wouldn't have to pull away from one another, their lips giving off that suction sound like two sets of hungry plungers.

"Miles?"

"Mmmhmm," he answered, still hungry for more of her.

"I need to ask you something. Something that's been bothering me."

"Okay shoot."

"I wanna know where you're gettin' all this money."

"What money?"

"This money . . ." Bambi brushed the dashboard with her fingertips. "This money." Now she pinched the short skirt she was wearing. Then she flaunted her engagement ring before him. "And *this* money. I know you do something with the Marines-n-all, but I ain't stupid. I know Marines can't afford this stuff."

Bambi waited for an explanation. Miles turned to look towards the water, the reflections rippling like some kind of liquid mirror. He wasn't sure what to say.

"I hope you're not selling drugs," she continued. Miles sucked his teeth and said, "Nothing like that, Bambi."

"Then what?"

"How about we discuss it tomorrow?" He kissed her cheek. "Over dinner."

"I'd like that," she said. And she softened into his embrace, stretching across the front seat, caressing his thigh as she went back to kissing him.

Gus was spending these last hours, these hours which led up to Monday morning, cleaning the inside of the GMC Yukon. Only 2 weeks old and he was already doing the thorough shampoo and vacuum of the carpet and finishing the tan leather seats. At five o'clock Monday morning he'd be meeting with Sonny to bring the gray pick-up truck to Hol-

brook where it would sit parked at the local 7-Eleven, not far
from the L.I.E. In the meantime, coffee kept him amped and
cleaning helped to ease his nerves. Suddenly, something
that sounded so easy was giving him the willies.

While Elvis was under the gun, while Miles was smooching
with Bambi, and while Gus was busy cleaning imaginary filth,
Sonny was on the phone with his sister Charlene. These were
off-hours at the base, a time she generally used to read, write
or exercise. Part goal-achieving and part tension-relieving.

"I just wanna say I'm real proud of you sis. I'll admit I was
jealous at one time. You're doin' somethin' I couldn't. But
now when I look back I can see I was just being big headed.
Maybe the Corps just wasn't for me and that drill instructor
Thor was the messenger, the message being: get out and get
your store for you. Ya mean?" Charlene had earned her pro-
motion to corporal and Sonny had called to congratulate her.
"What's this ya mean stuff, Sonny? You never talked like
this. What, are you gettin' all *street* now that you're out of the
military? Pickin' up bad habits from losers?"

"Maybe you're right sis. Sometimes I don't know who I
wanna be anymore. Some days I wanna be a thug. Others I
wanna be a successful entrepreneur. Others I just wanna disappear."

"Are you cryin', Sonny? Sonny?"

"Nah . . . I'm good," he lied.

"Sonny, you're startin' to worry me. Really. You've got
so much potential, so many dreams. Sounds like you just
need a little guidance. A lot of times the best of us don't like
to admit the truth, how we need direction in life. Like a ship
needs a destination, or like a pirate needs a treasure map.
Without that, we're lost."

"I know, I know. Anyhow I just wanted to call to congratulate you . . . *Corporal*."

"Thank you, Sonny. It means a lot to me that you care.
Call me anytime, won't you? Whenever you need an ear or a
shoulder to cry on, I'm here."

"Thanks, sis."

* * *

"You know, I didn't wanna say this before Miles, but I was startin' to think Elvis was fishy, especially how he's been actin' lately. Like he been doin' drugs."

"I seen that too, Sonny. Like, yesterday at Well's. Dude's eyes were all red-n-shit, nah mean?"

"Maybe he needed sleep or somethin'," Miles said in defense of Elvis. "I mean, how can you fault a dude who was thorough enough to help us pull off that Bling lick?"

Both Sonny and Gus held the same expression, knowing damned good and well that the man's actions outdid any such small deficiency such as showing up late.

"Think about it, maybe he had a major problem gettin' out here. A traffic ticket, even."

"But he can't stop this move we 'bout to make," said Gus. "Oh, hell no. If he don't show up soon, we move out and do this shit ourselves. Instead of four cars on the expressway, we'll just have three. Besides one less man means more money for all of us."

"Oh shit," said Sonny. "I never thought about it that way."

"Now you mention it, I hope he don't show up. Fuck them two-way radios. We just gonna have to go hard." Gus pulled back the slide on his weapon, the gun metal's friction filling the Mercedes with the reminders of mortal danger.

"I sure like this ride Miles," Sonny said with his eyes canvassing the lights, gauges and devices on the dashboard.

"Don't get too comfy, dog. You'll be in that pick-up in a few minutes."

The three conspirators drank coffee and discussed the hit, parked there in the 7-Eleven lot, just a few blocks north of the L.I.E.'s Holbrook exit. Sonny and Gus had made an earlier run, driving out to Long Island to park one of the vehicles, then they drove back home, rested, and headed back out, Miles included, all in separate vehicles in a sort of motor-cade of criminal intent. The Mercedes was parked on a sub-urban street in Deer Park, and the three proceeded further into Long Island to assume their places. Gus was in the blue Ford Escort. Sonny was in the gray pick-up truck. Both of them waiting at the filling station close to where their target would be entering the expressway. Meanwhile, Miles went deeper into Holbrook, a block away from the corporate headquarters of Harry Winston. Without the binoculars, Miles could still see the entrance to the office building, where the rent-a-cop would make his rounds, and where, soon, Matthew Katz the jewelry salesman would be coming to pick up the African Queen diamond.

Elvis was and wasn't a prisoner. He'd picked up the rental from 125th Street the night before and had it gassed up and prepared for the day's run. It had been parked out in front of Melanie's place when Rose showed up.

Now, at minutes to twelve, Elvis was playing tour guide, driving a Chevy Caprice with a worn, burgundy exterior and a dashboard with most everything missing but the necessities. Rose was in the passenger's seat listening to Elvis' rendition of how this hit would go down, making mental notes of the details about the Jew, about the office building in Holbrook and about the 20-minute window inside which Miles and friends would be working out on the Long Island Expressway.

"But I'm being honest with you Rose. I don't think this'll go down right without me, the fourth man. They're expectin' me."

Rose had seen through his lie earlier, but this time if Elvis was lying he was doing a damned good job at it. "There they are, see? Over by the telephones." Elvis was pointing out Gus and Sonny sitting in the pickup and the Escort at the filling station. Elvis steered the Chevy into the filling station on the eastbound side of the L.I.E. Behind him were the reputed Hot Girls. All of them on GSXR 1100's. Nothing like a Hell's Angels gang, the Hot Girls were attractive enough to be Beth Ann models. Misa was out in front. The leader amongst the girls and the love of Rose's life. Behind Misa was Charmaine, the rough but not necessarily smart girl who always wore her diamond bracelet (whether during fight or flight) and a skull cap over her shoulder length hair.

Trina was juxtaposed by Charmaine. She was the sexy one who loved furs, skimpy outfits and women, probably as much as she loved men. Iris and Liza Fuentez were on the same bike, 19 year old twins who were pretty enough to be actresses, songbirds, dancers or fashion models. Both from the suppressive environment of Spanish Harlem, where the buildings are just as crammed together as the families living in them. Bringing up the rear was the fifth Hot Girl, Chanté. She was the darkest of the group, with that straight-from-the-jungle look, wild dreads sprouting in every which way (like stubby, limp asparagus stalks) and the fashionable camouflage outfit to fit her attitude. Chanté also held the title as the fastest biker on Rockaway Boulevard. A race that earned her 3 grand within the past month.

"Tell you what," Rose said. "You go on with your little jewelry heist. But I'm gonna tell you now . . . we'll be on your ass every step of the way . . . up until you get this so-called African Queen diamond. If anything even *smells* funny, all I'll do is turn my head . . . see that army behind us? They'll put so many holes in you, you won't remember where to shit from." Rose started to get out of the car.

"How you gonna get the diamond?" Elvis asked.

"Let me worry about that." Rose shut the door.

CHAPTER THIRTEEN

A bit oafish, Matthew Katz ambled out of the front lobby of Harry Winston, attaché case in hand. His tweed blazer covered his wrist just enough to conceal the handcuffs. The moment Matthew descended the steps he reached in his blazer and pulled out a paperback book. *STAR WARS, Captain's Log XXIVX, Adventures on Uranus.* With his one hand he opened the book to a dog-eared page and began reading on the way to the Volkswagen. It was parked in the visitors' area, just past where the executives' spaces were filled. Lexus. Mercedes. Cadillac. Lexus. Porsche. Porsche. Somebody in Harry Wintson was stacking chips.

Matthew reached the car, put the book in the hand holding the attaché case and held it up, still reading as his free hand reached in his pants pocket for car keys. Matthew Katz, the Trekkie.

His hand had eyes of its own, however blindly, making one attempt after the next to fit the key into the door. A short time passed when Matthew had to shake himself free from the fix he had on the book. Captain Kirk had been threatened by a Klingon's laser fire while he was bunkered in a sand trap with his latest nubile love interest, Princess Shakeera from the planet Uranus. Kirk was doing four things at once; ducking enemy fire, radioing Scotty for help, romancing Princess Shakeera, and keeping his hair perfect all-the-while. Kirk had kissed the princess for the first time when

Matthew turned his attention to the keyhole. Why did Kirk always have to interrupt the action with this romance stuff? Matthew would have to write a letter to the authors about that. Finally inside the blue bug, Matthew swung the attaché case over into the passenger's seat . . . his hand with it, and he took another minute to finish reading the page. *"Maybe if that laser hit him in the nose he'd stick to the business at hand,"* Matthew thought.

Matthew dog eared the page again, put the book down and fixed his yarmulke—as if he had to look good for this drive back to the city. Then he started the car and adjusted his glasses. On his way out of the lot, Matthew waved at the rent-a-cop and turned on the oldies station. His head immediately started bopping and his high nasal voice began the sing-a-long with the radio.

"YOU GOTTA TREAT HER LIKE A LADY . . . DO THE BEST YOU CAN DO . . . YOU GOTTA TREAT HER LIKE A LADY! SHE'LL GIVE IN TO YOU! AWW! LOOK AND SEE! YOU KNOW WHAT I MEAN!"

Matthew came to a red light and took up the book again, trying to see if Captain Kirk would get hit by a laser beam or if Scotty would beam him up in time. Before long an angry driver blew his horn while simultaneously cutting around the bug. Matthew rolled his eyes at the driver's impatience. He said, *"Road rage isn't Godly."* And he said it as if to put a curse on the offender. With clenched teeth, Matthew resumed driving before the light turned red again. It was his world and nothing else mattered. Just as he passed the 7-Eleven, he began singing again. Doing the twist now, as if the two of them (Matthew and Chubby) were there in the car's cramped space together, performing in that give-and-take way that entertainers do with the whole call and response bit. The entrance to the L.I.E. approached. He strapped on his seatbelt, manipulating the attaché as he did, and he guided the Volkswagen down the entrance ramp. It was nearly twelve noon. Very little traffic, just as Matthew boasted about at the last Diamond Club gathering.

"WHAT THE WORLD NEEDS NOW, IS LOVE, SWEET LOVE. IT'S THE ONLY THING THAT THERE'S JUST TOO LITTLE OF . . ." Matthew Katz as Dionne Warwick.

The three rentals were directly behind the Volkswagen now. Sonny was in the grey pick-up, to the left. Gus was in the blue Ford Escort, directly behind the Volkswagen. Miles was not happy about the two-tone Buick Skylark he drove. It was rusted along the edges and had some rear-end damage. If Elvis wasn't gonna go along with this, the least he could've done was leave the Chevy for Miles. It was a stronger car . . . more dependable than the Buick. Miles told himself: "If Bambi ever caught me in this heap of trash . . ." Since there were no 2-way radios to communicate amongst one another, the plan was to stay focused on the target. Once everyone passed the highway patrol car (known to hide behind the line of trees) just after the Central Islip entrance, they'd close in. Car radios off. Seat belts on. Focused.

"SINCE YOU'VE BEEN GONE!
ALL THAT'S LEFT IS A BAND OF GOLD!
ALL THAT'S LEFT OF THE DREAMS
I HOLD . . . IS A BAND OF GOLD . . . !!"

Matthew was on a roll, but in more ways than one. There was a thud to the left of him and his body jerked. His immediate reflex was to steer left and stay on the road. He tried, but his car seemed to be on its own. He looked left to see what hit him, but within the space of a second another thud hit him from the right, jerking him again. Matthew was instantly dizzy. His glasses fell to the side and he subconsciously reached up to his head, maybe to keep it intact. Now there was a thud from behind, almost sending him crashing into the windshield. There was rubber burning somewhere. Smoke. Matthew looked left. A pick up truck was practically kissing up to his car. On the right, a red Buick was doing the same. The rear view mirror was thrown out of whack, so he couldn't see behind. This road-rage stuff was getting out of hand. His instincts made him fight back, swinging the steering wheel back and forth, back and forth. He felt his car banging relentlessly into the other vehicles, but they shouldn'ta been crowding him! Finally, Matthew jammed his foot into the accelerator. The bug shot out ahead of the three car enclosure, and with no other cars on the road to slow him, he made a clean break, moving further and further out of his assailant's reach.

Elvis had to act fast. This plan was too sweet to go sour this easy. He had been gaining on the four vehicles and recognized that the three cars had the target corralled, and how the smaller car was then muscling its way out of the trap, picking up speed like a rascally rodent.

Elvis could not let this happen. He couldn't let this guy get away, no matter what. Not only was Rose and his army of female bikers somewhere watching all of this, but the only thing Elvis had to bargain with, the only thing that might save his ass, was to complete the hit successfully. Essentially, he'd really be saving *all* their asses in doing so.

"Damn it!" Miles shouted alone in the Buick. He didn't expect that this little critter of a car would be able to outrun his crew or that its driver, the salesman, the Star Trek fanatic, would be this difficult to deal with. And now, Miles saw the Chevy (ELVIS!) to the left of them, racing up the fast lane to catch the Volkswagen. It was mere seconds before Elvis caught up to the Trekkie in the Chevy Caprice, law enforcement's vehicle of choice.

Elvis lined up the Chevy with the Volkswagen. The differences in the vehicles were immediately obvious, almost two to one in size and power. There was a brief second when the bug's driver looked over and shared a look with Elvis. Then he looked again, this time sticking his tongue out. Taunting him. Elvis needed no further encouragement. He whipped the steering wheel to the right, forcing the Chevy to slam its body into the Volkswagen. The Volkswagen swerved out of control. It turned into a wild blue spinning top and flipped over and over until it came to a stop in the middle of the expressway. Miles cut away to the shoulder and Sonny skidded to a stop. But Gus couldn't get the Escort to slow. The brakes gave. Instantly and violently, the Ford Escort collided with the Volkswagen.

The area where the failed ambush happened was heavily wooded, lined with enough trees to block out much of the sky and all of the surrounding community. A guard rail divided the eastbound and westbound sides of the L.I.E. On the eastbound side, drivers were slowing, curious about the collision, gawking in disbelief but eventually continuing on their way.

In the meantime, despite the audience that was accumulating, Miles and Sonny pulled down their ski masks and in broad daylight sprinted toward the wreckage. The fumes of gasoline rose about the area and made their eyes tear.

Miles coughed and called out for Gus. Sonny ran ahead towards the overturned Bug. He looked in through the broken driver's side window to see Matthew Katz balled up like a fetus, bleeding heavily from the series of wounds across his face. He wasn't moving. But somewhere in that wreckage there was an attaché case. Sonny pushed at Matthew's body, hoping to free it. Hoping to at least see something.

"Yo! Sonny!! Gus is alive!" Miles was yelling from about 25 feet away. "Help me out over here!"

Sonny had turned his head towards Miles, trying to decide what was more important. The diamond or Gus.

Just then his wrist was gripped by Matthew Katz's outreached hand. The injured salesman made a desperate plea. "Help me . . ." His words were somewhat lifeless, poking eerily at Sonny's conscience. It was an instant that helped Sonny to make up his mind. He snatched his wrist away, and he rushed over to Miles.

The impact of the collision had sent Gus into the windshield of the Escort. By the time Sonny came over to help, Miles already had his hands bloodied in an attempt to help

Gus from the mangled, smoking vehicle. Sonny tried to keep his expression to himself, knowing that Gus was already in a bad way. No sense in adding any more discouragement to an already fucked-up situation. His friend's skull had been through grave trauma. His eyes were partially rolled back within their sockets. Blood was everywhere. Either Gus was dead, or he was about to die.

"He's breathing. Help me get him out."

Sonny was stuck in the moment; unsure of what (if any) help they could afford Gus now. Miles turned to look over his shoulder. A threatening look as he pulled at Gus' limp body. Sonny went ahead and assisted, wanting to satisfy Miles, but knowing the efforts would be futile. Besides, there was still the diamond to go after.

They managed to get Gus out of the wreckage and carried him as best they could until they laid him over the backseat of the Buick. Just the smell of Gus' blood turned Sonny's stomach; plus the look on Miles' face was disturbing his sense of what was and what wasn't important here.

"Oh shit! Look!" Sonny called attention to the wrecked Volkswagen. Elvis was over there with the Trekkie, already dragging the guy halfway out of the vehicle. Miles felt the same way Sonny did under the circumstances, that there was deceit in the air. He was caught between helping Gus and dealing with Elvis.

CHAPTER FOURTEEN

Miles drove the Buick to the very next exit close by where he'd parked the Mercedes on a quiet residential street. The Buick, pick-up truck, Ford Escort and Chevy Caprice were all rented under phony names using phony ID's. So leaving them behind on the L.I.E. or ditching them, as Miles did with the Buick Skylark, was no loss and left no strings attached to the three.

Just as quick as they got rid of the Buick, they loaded up in Miles's Mercedes and headed west for home, complying with the speed limit. Not a word was spoken. However, just before they crossed the Whitestone Bridge, Miles steered into a service road, which led to the graveled area and grassy sprawl overlooking the broad inlet of the Long Island Sound. He threw the car into park, shut off the engine and fitfully got out.

Sonny sat in the passenger's seat, watched Miles for a moment and then squeezed his thumb and forefingers against his closed eyelids as though pinching away tears. By the time he opened his eyes, Miles was close to the decline of large rocks that marked the coastline. Miles was on his knees, one hand on the earth before him and the other holding his stomach as he heaved his latest meal onto the ground. Sonny watched his friend, feeling the same pain and loss, his stomach a little nauseous as well. Elvis was there in the backseat, his head tilted back, looking up in a stupor.

Sonny gave Miles a couple of minutes alone before he looked back at Elvis. Both eventually left the car to approach Miles.

Miles was sick to his stomach. It wasn't just that they'd been robbed, that they wouldn't realize the big payoff he'd planned for and dreamed about. It was Gus. It was Gus' blood on his hands. Still on his hands. It was the ever-fresh memory of Gus' broken body as he and Sonny carried him; as he and Sonny and Elvis left him. Just like that, they'd left their comrade dead at the scene of their crime.

His stomach mostly emptied, Miles spit the residue left in his mouth and any other offensive taste left on his tongue. His body felt queasy and unbalanced, but relieved just the same. Miles was aware that the two others were standing behind him, and when he was able, he got up, wiped his mouth and looked at both of them. The way he turned his eyes from Sonny to Elvis was a slow motion exercise, with a blink in between until he finally read Elvis.

"What happened out there, Elvis? You were late. You didn't call or page. And it's obvious that somebody knew exactly . . . *specifically* where we'd be and what we were after. They had us *timed*, goddamn it!" Miles was feet away from Elvis in a tense moment, the three of them armed and nervous with both fear and rage.

"Alright, calm down Miles. It's not what you think."

"*What's* not what I think? What the fuck are you talkin' about?"

"Could you calm down a sec? At least gimme' a chance to explain." Elvis had his arms extended slightly, a pleading gesture. Miles was hungry to learn what went wrong, to the point that he shivered with anticipation. "Last night I was with Melanie after I picked up the Chevy and the 2-ways, out of nowhere they bum-rushed the front door, all of 'em had guns-n-shit."

"Who?"

Elvis wagged his head. "You're not gonna believe this. It was Rose. The dude I told you about."

"The one you sell guns for?"

"Yes. He had the rapper with 'em, and a few of his girls, the same ones that was with him back on the expressway . . ."

"The rapper?"

"The *rapper.* Bling. The one we robbed. Rose was somehow involved with Bling's brother Bingo. Bingo is a number-runner and, if I got it correct, Rose gets a piece of that action."

"And you didn't know this when we did the lick?"

"No. I only learned this last night."

"So how that end up with us losin' the diamond?"

"Rose wanted the jewels back. I told 'em we didn't have 'em. We sold 'em. He asked me about the money." Elvis read the expression on Miles' face, no doubt wondering why Elvis gave up the information so easily. "He had a gun on me! About to kill me! I was beggin' for my *fuckin'* life! I told Rose we had somethin' goin' down."

Miles pulled out his M-1 pistol and released the safety, pointing it at Elvis.

"Miles!" Sonny shouted. "Miles!!"

"This was a setup, Sonny. Probably from the door. Elvis was the one to tell us about that rap Motha-fucka. And now, after we make the lick, he comes up with this cock-n-bull story about some Rose dude. They probably had us setup the whole fuckin' time! Just to get their hands on shit we was doin'. How else you explain this?" Miles had Sonny's attention.

"Miles, it does make sense. I mean, it ain't no coincidence he did time down on Parris Island or that he went through the same shit we did." Now Sonny found himself sticking up for Elvis as Miles had earlier on that morning. "Don't you remember when you first brought Elvis in the game? *You* were the one who convinced us he was good money. Now you wanna switch up! Now you want a murder rap?"

"GUS IS DEAD! OUR MONEY IS GONE! ALL OUR WORK FOR NOTHIN'!" Miles roared and fired his weapon, empting its 15 rounds into the sky until he could fire no more. The mass of water and the stream of cars passing by the gunshots seemed to swallow the sounds of the gunshots, as if they never happened. Elvis could've collapsed there on the grass, realizing how his life hung in the balance again, twice within 24 hours.

There was no way on God's green earth that Miles would seek revenge or attack Rose and his girls for what they'd done. After all, if the rapper dude was an investment, then Rose was more-or-less looking after his investment. In his right mind, Miles understood the man's pain. He stole from those who stole from him. It made no sense whatsoever to retaliate now. The possibility would (no doubt) end up with more dead bodies.

The defeated trio returned home that evening. Fortunately there were shoulders to cry on, and wanton thighs that led to familiar entries - no less than sleeves in which to empty their frustrations.

Sonny stopped by the projects to see Dori. She had always been convenient for a booty call in the past. But this evening was different. He actually needed her. He sugarcoated the occasion with all sorts of promises and exclamations about how he "missed her," and "how she meant the world to him." But in the end, after he'd shot his load where he wanted, he quickly felt out of place. He didn't love this girl. And he certainly didn't feel right lying there naked with her in his arms. The uneasiness coupled with the day's events was enough to fall asleep and hope it was all a bad dream.

Elvis returned to Melanie's place to find her landlord threatening him. The landlord told him to get off of her property or else she'd turn him in. He couldn't imagine what she meant, not until she murmured something about *using all kinds of drugs* in her house and *destroying her property.* The woman was saying this, and cursing, all while she was carrying Melanie's things out through the broken door to the studio. That, Elvis realized, would account for all the mess out on the sidewalk. The lamps and boxes of clothes and dishes were mere junk at first. But the moment Elvis saw what was happening, the belongings immediately became familiar.

He wasn't standing there long before a taxi pulled up curbside. It was Melanie, exasperated but ecstatic to see Elvis.

"She's throwin' us out, Elvis. I can't even take it to the police." Elvis hugged Melanie. The driver helped the two load what they could into the cab and they headed to Manhattan to rent a room at the Ramada Hotel on 57th street. They figured on this "being home" until the real estate broker came through and completed their deal on the penthouse.

By the time they settled in with all of Melanie's clothes, cosmetics and other personal effects cluttering room 401, they rushed to embrace. That they were both emitting musky, offensive odors from the day was of little consequence in this time rife with frustration. Elvis needed someone, somewhere or something in which to repent just as much as Melanie needed to feel his force and to exert her own suppressed emotions. Essentially, he needed to plunge into her and she felt that strong need to receive him. While in their complicated funk, Melanie spoke softly in his ear.

"El?" She said, invoking the pet name they were accustomed to. "Mel" was his pet name for her. "You want some blow?"

"Later. Right now I want you." And Elvis submerged himself in a compassionate kiss that began at her lips and moved along her salty neck and collarbone.

As they warmed with desire Elvis pressed into her, backing her to a wall. His hands groped at Melanie, almost forcefully massaging her ass and breasts. Her tolerance was measured in moans and whimpers fed directly into his mouth. The friction increased and the intensity turned near violent. Elvis spun Melanie and she spontaneously slammed her palms against the wall as he did. His body to hers, Elvis worked his hands underneath her blouse, grabbing at her mounds of wanton flesh. Then he abruptly pulled her spandex pants to her thighs and turned her body so that it slumped over onto the bureau and mirror combination nearby.

Somewhat caught up in the madness of passion, Melanie's panting and begging encouraged Elvis in his hurry to be inside of her. The mirror before him infused his ego with a hungry new life.

"Come on, come on, come on," she gasped in earnest, pulling at Elvis' senses by her consent, compelling his actions by her sputtering impulsivity. Without his hands on her, Melanie knew it wouldn't be long. Her own walls were slick and gooey with anticipation, adding to the repulsive body odors already in the midst. When his hands grabbed her again, this time by the hips, Melanie could feel him filling her before he actually had. It made her breathing erratic, a force and turmoil inside her own body, heaving as if she was in between relay races.

Finally, he inserted himself. He looked down at her head of hair scattered and hiding her face, her bare back rising and falling on the surface of the bureau and her ass cheeks between which he was buried. Elvis knew immediately that this instant was more about him than her. More about the release of his pent up anguish than her need for attention or affection.

Love was a distant memory as Elvis plunged into Melanie. This had nothing at all to do with the future or their relationship. This had everything to do with how he felt right now. Melanie cried out sporadically as Elvis took her with authority. You'd think she was dying. In his quest he grunted and hummed, adding to his part in an aggressive animal-driven duet. You'd think he was having a heart attack.

When it was over Elvis fell over on top of Melanie. She could feel his heart banging at her back, the spasms of his finale still throbbing and twitching inside of her. Their breathing eventually steadied and their bodies became lifeless, relaxed slabs of tenderized meat.

* * *

2 am Tuesday morning woke Miles with the annoying beeping of his two-way pager. Once his eyes focused he read the digital screen. **"CALL ME IMMEDIATELY. GOOD NEWS."**

He had kept his date with Bambi and instead of telling her the truth, he said he *"bought and sold precious jewels."* At least (he rationalized) that was *half the truth.* Whatever he did manage to tell her only romanced her and further bonded them. Her eyes were more intoxicated by him as they sat over dinner. Her thoughts were satisfied; knowing now that her future was secure. No, she didn't find that doctor, that dentist or that lawyer that Daddy motivated her to find. But Miles would pass the test as acceptable. Plus Daddy said he liked Miles.

So many right signals came at her that night. Bambi wanted to reciprocate. And there was something about Miles, how he appeared, like he needed attention.

"Let's go to your place," Bambi suggested, not willing to spend one more session in a motel or hotel. Not willing to satisfy him as she had in the backseat of his Mercedes. This time she wanted something real . . . something meaningful.

Those words were the music to his ears, for Bambi to be direct, virtually saying she wanted to do the give-and-take, and that she wanted to do it now. There was no way Miles could take Bambi back to the realities of his mother's place back on Warburton Avenue in Yonkers. And he had been meaning to stop by Gus' place in any event. So, as awkward as it felt, Miles drove Bambi to the South Bronx where Gus lived in the finished basement of a brownstone building. Miles had the spare key "just in case," as Gus would put it. This moment and this day marked no greater alternative. No more pressing a need. When they arrived at Gus' crib, the entry was dark. The lamp over the door was off, leaving only reflections of the night to light their way into the basement.

"Careful," Miles said, as he wondered what the place

might look like; if it'd be different then when he'd last been there, perhaps messy enough to smother his plans for intimacy with Bambi.

"Isn't there a light in here?" Bambi asked, not wanting to budge.

Curiosity taunted her while a ghost, (Gus' ghost) pulled at Miles. It sucked all the spirit from the occasion.

"Now you know," Miles said, easing up behind Bambi. His arms cuddling her with assurance. "We don't need lights for what we 'bout to do." He bullshitted his way past the insecurity and turned Bambi to face him. He kissed her with an intensity unlike before. Not hard, but full of meaning and purpose.

Then with the soft outside light cast down through the basement window, Miles guided Bambi to the bed and lowered her onto her back, kissing her all the while. As he kept contact, her eyes caught in his, Miles knew that Bambi was his cushion at the worst of times as well as she would be his sharing partner during the lean moments of life. When his days were dark with misery she'd be his beacon of light and his breath of fresh air. Miles looked at Bambi as the willing, cooperative woman that he'd spend the rest of his life with. She was his diamond, his riches and his destiny. She was who he'd achieve for and enjoy success with. His companion. The love of his life. The mother-to-be of his children. With every fiber of his being, Miles made love to Bambi. His crying made her cry, and the loving was that much more important. He surrendered all control, all protection and all risk to his heart, which he followed until it was all over and he was spent.

When Elvis' message came over the two-way Miles had his arms wrapped warmly around his love, a position he had told himself to keep until he couldn't any longer. That position, she with her back to him, body to body, with his arms enfolded around her, his hands cupping her breasts, was his Utopia. His perfect world.

"This shit better be *real good*," Miles said in a sedate

voice into the telephone. He could smell Gus' essence on the mouthpiece.

"He needs us. He wants to deal."

"Who?"

"Rose."

CHAPTER FIFTEEN

Miles wanted to get over to Elvis so fast that he thought about leaving Bambi at the apartment. But he compromised; he asked her to get dressed, and used the down-time to get Sonny on the phone and have him ready so that he could swing by to pick him up.

"It's business, baby." Miles kissed Bambi upon her exodus from the Mercedes. "I had a good time."

"Me, too. See you later?" Bambi's eyes were glassy and dreamy.

"Count on it," Miles replied. Then he did a careful 50 miles per hour up the Bronx River Parkway to pick up Sonny.

"What'd he mean, 'Rose wants to deal?' " asked Miles as soon as Sonny loaded into the passenger seat. It was close to 3 in the morning, the night pushing towards a new day.

"I don't really know. But whatever he wants to work out is better than nothin' at all."

"True that." A silence squeezed into their conversation.

"You thinkin' about Gus?"

"I can't get him off my mind." Miles made the understatement realizing how his spending time there with Bambi was something like taboo. "That was my dog, Sonny. I don't know anyone who'd step out there like he has for me. He got that scar lookin' out for me."

"I never did find out how he got that scar. What happened?"

"They worked him over. The day he charged at 'em, when

they were shouting at me n' shit. We both got taken to an
empty office and a group of drill instructors started beatin' us
down. Body shots. Smackin' us. Stuff so we wouldn't bleed.
But Gus fought back. He kept attackin'. So they all jumped
him."

"Where were you?"

"Two of 'em took me to a bathroom. Jammed a chair under the doorknob. All I could hear was yellin'. I think Gus
hit a sharp edge or somethin'. A whole month passed. Next
thing I know he walked in the unit where recruits are discharged. I didn't think I'd see him again."

"Damn. Y'all had it ten times worse than me." Sonny
wagged his head and stared off into nothingness where road-
side forests gave way to a clear view of the Hudson River and
eventually the skyline of Manhattan.

"That's why we gotta live for him. We gotta get paid, otherwise it was all for nothin'.'"

"Word. What do you think they did with Gus?"

"They'll check his ID, try to contact his family."

"Wasn't his father his only family?"

"Yeah. And he's locked up. So as soon as we can we gotta
step up like we some old Marine Corps buddies. We'll offer
to handle funeral services and whatnot."

"Phew. I'm glad you said that. I didn't think you were
gonna just leave Gus out there, deserted."

"Never that."

"Where we goin' anyway?"

"Elvis is stayin' downtown at the Ramada on Fifty-seventh."

"What about Rose?"

Miles shrugged. "It's their show at this point. I'm down
with whatever they propose."

"You still think Elvis is in on it, don't you."

"I don't know *what* to think anymore, Sonny. Life just
ain't all that predictable no more."

Elvis was waiting down in the lobby when the Mercedes
rolled up. He wasted no time getting in.

"Harlem. One Twenty Third Street."

"What's up there?"

"That's where he wants to meet."

Miles made a U-turn and shot down 57th for the West Side Highway. It was only two exits north to 125th street.

"Did he say what kind of deal he wants to work out?" Miles asked.

"He didn't say and I didn't ask. He just said bring your friends and let's talk."

"Think this is another ambush?" Sonny's inquiry was directed at Miles.

"Well, worst case scenario . . . we're ready, aren't we?" Sonny's firearm suddenly felt like a brick at the small of his back. It was clear by the activity on the L.I.E., how those women just snatched the attaché case, that they would never be ready for this Rose dude.

"Yeah, of course," Sonny lied.

Once they turned from the highway and onto the off ramp, Elvis paged Rose. The discussion was short.

"He said to pull up to the corner of One twenty third and Manhattan, outside of Perk's," Elvis said when he flipped the cell phone shut. Miles and Sonny traded that helpless expression again as they cruised past the Cotton Club, then M&G's Diner, and up to a parked position outside of Perk's. The club was closed but a couple of people were still inside cleaning up.

The streets were empty of people and a soft wind ruffled leaves on the few trees that lined the edges of the area's sidewalks. The only other movement was a homeless man straggling along; his eyes were as dilated as his clothes were weak of color or life. He had a hat on, the look reminiscent of an old war hero, one of the "colored" ones who were pushed to the front lines.

It was surreal when the scruffy fellow approached the passenger side of the Mercedes and knocked on the window. The man's unkempt appearance startled the young team and they tried to ignore him, hoping he'd go away.

Sonny sucked his teeth and said, "Gimme a dollar so I can get rid of this fool."

"Give you a dollar? You got money."

"Yeah, but it's your window he's knockin' at."

"Sonny, just give the dude a dollar! *Damn!*"

"Here," Elvis whipped out a five dollar bill. "Don't look at me funny, that's the smallest bill I got."

Even in their misery the guys had spending money that a hard-working man would envy.

Miles reached down to his door panel for the button to lower the window where Sonny sat with the bill in hand. Immediately, the beggar reached in the car and snatched the money from Sonny's hand. The man's odors quickly sent evidence of days'-old funk.

"Thanks. You dudes here for Rose?" His voice was like a whisper, one that was raspy and odorous as well. But the mention of Rose shocked them.

"Yeah," Elvis said, sensing that this was the contact. The others tried to think past their disbelief.

"Well, I'm s'pose to watch your car. He waitin' over in there." The man pointed to the apartment building on the corner, adjacent to where they were parked.

"I'm gonna need another five, too. Insurance."

Elvis rolled his eyes, thinking the first five was already considered insurance. He paid him as the three got out of the car.

They approached the urine-stenched walkway that led to a glass-enclosed foyer. Under a depressing low-wattage light bulb, one of Rose's girls stood waiting. Another was inside of an innermost glass door.

"A welcome party, huh?" Miles said as they stepped into the foyer, almost filling it to capacity. Elvis wondered why he'd never gone through these procedures before and he shrugged at Miles when the girl began a body search.

"I'll hold this," said the screener, sticking Miles's pistol in her own waistband. She also took weapons from Sonny and Elvis, changing their attitudes to concern. Humbled, the three were let in the second door and led through a short lobby and the hallway where apartment 1B was located.

Another of Rose's girls opened that door after a coded knock.

"They clean?"

"They are now," the dark skinned woman answered, opening her jacket to reveal three weapons in her waistband.

All parties entered the apartment. It was swanky; a world away from how the outside of the building appeared, its facade in need of steam cleaning and the walk-up littered.

"Welcome to my home," Rose said, sitting between two women on a lime green leather couch. He was watching MS-NBC news on a wide flat screen monitor mounted on the wall over an entertainment center and service bar to the side. "Get them drinks, Iris," Rose directed. The Latina was fit for a movie role or a fashion advertisement. Her auburn hair was pulled back into a ponytail and she wore a soft yellow halter top and pants. Iris was barefoot, they noticed, as she stepped up to ask what they wanted to drink. Her smiling eyes quickly eased the crew, as if they were family. "Come on over . . . have a seat. Relax, it's cool."

Miles and Sonny made questioning eyes at one another. Elvis joined in, too, expressing that he knew it'd be this way all along. Still suspicious, the guys took a seat; aware that 5 armed and dangerous women were there amongst them to maintain order on behalf of Rose.

"You look surprised . . . edgy. Don't be so wired up." Easy for Rose to say.

"How would you be?" Miles asked. "If 5 women with guns came up and took the future right out of your hands?"

"Oh, that." Rose turned to whisper to the woman with a diamond bracelet. She got up and reached behind the service bar. "Would you feel better if I returned it to you? I mean, I wouldn't wanna be the one to steal your future." As Rose said this, the Milky Way–brown cutie, also barefoot in FUBU casuals, came and handed Miles the attaché case. Her top was embroidered with her name: "Charmaine." The disbelief that washed over the faces of Miles, Sonny and Elvis was unpreventable. Miles noticed that the cuff had been removed and the leather case picked open. He wanted to check inside, but didn't want to be so bold or to question Rose's credibility.

"Go ahead," Rose said. "Open it."

Miles hesitated; another bout with disbelief, then he finally flipped the attaché case open. A small box set in the center of the attaché case supported by horizontal and vertical Styrofoam blocks. This was the first time any of them, Sonny, Elvis or Miles, saw what was inside. So all eyes pulled at the lid to the casing. Miles closed his eyes briefly, saying a short prayer, hoping that this was not a joke and that the African Queen diamond would be there.

Miles looked at Rose, to maybe catch a disingenuous expression. There was none. Rose merely nodded, urging Miles to proceed as directed.

The instant that light was let in, that same light was reflected, sparkling and glistening off of the diamond. The breath pushed out of Miles' lungs to see the small, pear-shaped jewel with its beveled corners, its patterns of hearts and arrows. Miles recalled how Sasha Franco called this emerald, *"One of the largest and finest in the world . . . One of South Africa's greatest assets."* But Miles saw more than just shimmering brilliance before him. He saw Bambi in a wedding gown, looking extravagant, waiting for him to say, "I do" with her doe-eyes under a sheer veil. He saw the clothing business he and Sonny would open in the White Plains Galleria. He saw a big house to where he'd move, maybe bringing his mother with him. He'd even move her to a house next door if she wanted. There was that much money in his hands.

"Nice rock you all got there. I almost felt guilty about taking it from you." Rose muted the sound on the T.V. screen as he spoke. "Looks like you all really did your homework. Congratulations."

Sonny wanted to get to the point. "What's the catch?" he asked.

"Well let's see," Rose said with his thinking man's pose. "You stole from Bling, so that means you stole from me.

You humiliated the rapper and his family and ahh . . . well let me do this . . . Let me introduce you to a couple of people I know. Maybe you'll understand the damage you did when you meet them."

Miles had no chance to object. There were already two men coming from another room. When Sonny recognized the two he wanted to disappear. Elvis felt his intestines churn. The three suddenly missed their guns very much.

Bling was just behind Buck and Nitro as they stepped into Rose's living room. The large bodyguards seethed in front of the three visitors, cracking their knuckles and grimacing at the temptation of getting retribution. The big men wore meshed wife beater tops, weight lifter pants and leather driving gloves folded back near the wrists.

"Rose, come on dude. Don't do this," Elvis pleaded.

"Buddy, you got shit a little backwards. It wasn't me who did anything. Now, you got your diamond back, so we really don't have anything more to discuss, do we?"

"Ah . . . Rose. Can we work somethin' out? Can we? It's in our best interests right now."

"You could be right about that Elvis."

Rose made Buck and Nitro back up. They ushered Bling to a table in the dining room nearby. "So now . . . what is it you wanna work out?" Elvis nudged Miles. There was silence.

"Okay. See, this rock that we took is worth at least two million," Miles said. "And I'm talkin' cash. All I gotta do is break off a partner and the other half is ours."

"I thought the rock was worth three million."

"It's worth three, but that doesn't mean we'll get three. I think the dude I deal with had to break it down in smaller parts."

"What's your deal with him?" Roses asked.

"Fifty-fifty."

"When's he payin'?"

"As soon as I bring the stone in. Usually on big jobs I make two cash pick-ups. This might take three or four."

"And what're you thinkin' of workin' out wit' me?"

"Uh, how about half of what we get?" Miles said.

Sonny's eyes bulged at Miles. But Miles gave Sonny a scolding look, urging him to keep his mouth shut. *Don't you realize the mess we're in?* Rose thought about the offer. "I'm thinking a third," Rose said. Miles thought Rose was crazy for accepting less until Rose said, "a third of the value." The room was silent again. Miles did the calculating. If the value was seven or eight million then Rose wanted 66 percent, or 666,000. Half of Miles' million dollar purse would mean $500,000. Essentially, Rose wanted over $150,000 more than what Miles offered.

Miles figured that the $666,000 split between him, Sonny, and Elvis would mean only $222,000 for each man. If Gus was figured in, with funeral arrangements and the money Miles wanted to put aside to help with the appeal for Gus' father, there might only be $200,000 left between them. Miles knew the eyes were on him. He was the man to propose the African Queen heist in the first place. He was the one who had the connect for cashing in the stone. A local fence would only be arrested if he presented such a fine stone. The reward was probably more than what the fence would pay anyhow.

Miles knew Elvis and Sonny were looking at him, concerned about their cut and their plans (for $300,000 to $500,000). He knew Rose was looking at him, expecting to come through on behalf of his organization, his rapper and various associates. Miles was also ever-aware of Buck and Nitro sitting to the far left at the dining table, eager to rip him and his boys apart like rottweilers would rip apart t-bone steaks. There was just one choice to make here, and it didn't take a chess master's mind to figure out. This was a life or death decision.

"First, I hope your, uh . . . *friends* over there, and you will accept our apologizes. I hope you realize we had no idea. If we did . . ."

"No need. I can handle them. Just tell me what you gonna do."

"One third," Miles finally said.

Tension freed in the air. Sonny deflated as if life was

sucked out of him. Elvis closed his eyes and said a personal prayer. Rose got up and shook Miles' hand.

"I'm glad we can work this out 'cause, for real? Them dudes over there is *hot* with you all."

"You sure you—" Miles was interrupted.

"I told you. Don't worry. I got that. Now when should I expect payment?"

"The guy I deal with will probably hit me with as much as I can handle. He just doesn't want me to be leavin' his spot with bulked up bags of cash."

"I'll send somebody with you."

"Nah, that's alright."

"I insist. Charmaine . . ." She strutted over from where she had been standing and whispering to Chanté. "You're goin' for a little ride. My man here is gonna take you downtown to see about some business."

"Not a problem. I'll be dressed in two minutes."

"Meanwhile, you two make yourselves at home. Liza's gonna take you across the hall to 1C. It's just like my spot so you'll be able to relax, kick back, whatever. Iris and Chanté will take care of you, see that you're comfortable."

Despite how attractive Iris and Chanté were, Elvis and Sonny already felt like prisoners. Sonny said, "You better get that money dog. Don't let 'em feed us to the lions."

"Don't worry son. I got you."

CHAPTER SIXTEEN

Some of the storefronts in the diamond district opened as early as 6:30 and 7am. But the mini-mall arrangement where Sasha Franco's enterprise was established didn't open until 9am. That left 5 hours before Miles would meet the jeweler and complete the transaction.

In the meantime, Miles spent an hour and a half assuring Sonny and Elvis across the hall in apartment 1C. At the same time he paged Sasha Franco one, two and even three times before the guy finally returned the call.

"What're you sleepin' under a rock?" Miles asked when Sasha finally picked up the phone.

"Are you crazy? I wait for your call twelve, thirteen, fourteen hours. Now you call me at five in the morning."

"I had problems."

"I heard. They played the incident on New York One all day. You have African Queen?" Sasha asked. Miles almost forgot that was the name of the diamond, having called Bambi that name for so long.

"Yeah. How early can we meet?"

"We cannot meet. Not now."

"What?!" Miles was immediately enraged.

"Everything different now. You killed two people. Police maybe come for you, for me—"

"Hey listen you." Miles didn't want to be so evil towards the jeweler. Didn't want to have to show his *other* side. Plus, the relationship had been so good up till this point. "Sasha, first of all, I don't know what you're talking about. I didn't kill anybody. And if I did, I wouldn't be foolish enough to discuss that over the phone. Second we have a *deal*. Now, I expect to meet with you this morning, same as before . . . cash."

"No deal."

Miles mumbled now, not wanting his buddies or Rose's girls to hear. "No deal huh? Okay Sasha, you leave me no other choice. I'm gonna meet with the folks at Harry Winston. Maybe they'll buy their own property back from me. Maybe I'll just go and get a reward for this beauty. Drop a certain name too."

"You wouldn't."

"Try me."

"Six-thirty. Four Seasons Hotel. On Fifty—"

"I know where it is. What room?"

"Penthouse one."

"Don't be late," Miles said, hanging up abruptly. Sonny and Elvis were on the couch, soaked into the comfort, already engaged with the accommodations, care of Chanté and Iris. Miles rolled his eyes, telling himself, "*if they only knew.*"

With an hour until the meeting, Miles and Charmaine left Harlem for Manhattan.

"So how long you been working for Rose?"

"A while," Charmaine said with no fluctuation in her voice.

"You like it?"

"It's a living," Charmaine said, her eyes on M&G's as they passed. Miles noticed, even by his glance, that her eyes twinkled.

"You wanna stop for a bite? Coffee?"

"Nah. That's alright." She flipped down the visor up in front of her, looking in the mirror to check her make up. The little she had on couldn't do too much more, she was already stunning.

"Where you from anyway?"

Charmaine rolled her eyes, flipped the visor shut and turned her body to face Miles.

"Listen here nigga, it's too early in the fuckin' morning for some lame I'd-like-to-get-to-know-you talk. NO . . . it's none-a-your-*business* where I'm from, what I do or how. I'm here to handle business for Rose . . ."

Miles cut in, "Like a soldier."

"You motha-fuckin' right. I'd *kill* for that nigga. I'd *die* for that nigga. Ain't nothin' about you impresses me. Matter of fact, stop the car," Charmaine said. Miles had just turned onto the ramp to take the West Side Highway downtown.

"What're you talking—?"

"I said stop the motha-fuckin' *car*," Charmaine commanded, pulling back the slide on her firearm and pressing it against his temple.

"Alright. *Alright already!*" Miles slowed to a stop on the entrance ramp. Charmaine got out of the passenger's seat and hopped in the back seat of the car.

"I was just tryin' to be nice," said Miles.

"Drive," Charmaine commanded.

Miles wagged his head, wondering how things had gone so foul so suddenly.

Concentrating on the business at hand, Miles still couldn't help but to spend his share, sight unseen. Already he knew he wouldn't be able to buy himself or his mother a house. At least he'd be able to afford the payments on something nice, maybe a town house for himself and Bambi, or maybe he could lease a two family house and rent out part of it for rental income.

However, the Galleria project was a definite. All he'd need is $100,000 for that. Along with Sonny's $100,000, they could lease a nice size space in a prime location, somewhere near the food court, and they'd fill it up with brand name urban wear. As much as the designers like NYCE, ECKO, Karl Kani, and Sean John were advertising on T.V. and in *The Source*, *Vibe* and *XXL* magazines, it was the locals in isolated areas ike Westchester County who would come scrambling to the Galleria for a 1st shot at the fad for the month. Most importantly, Miles would have a hundred thousand to secure a lifestyle suitable for his new wife. They could afford a child. Even two. They'd have a trust fund set aside for the child's schooling. Miles would buy a 2nd car, and he'd invest money in a nice professional demo so that record labels might at least listen to Bambi's talent. As Miles turned off the exit ramp and up 57th street, he let his mind wander and thought about renting out a club, maybe the world famous Copacabana, he'd pay for a nice showcase there and have a publicist invite a few dozen record executives.

It was pushing 6 o'clock now. There was time to spare, so Miles drove down to the Times Square area. He needed a travel bag for the cash. None of the stores were open there, so he went down 42nd. Fortunately, there was a street vendor who set up early. Miles bought two leather valises and headed back up towards The Four Seasons. He paid the doorman handsomely to watch his car and was joined by Charmaine as he strolled into the hotel lobby.

"Who's the girl?" Sasha asked.

"A friend."

"I only do business with you. Lose her."

"*Lose* her?" Charmaine said with a devilish gaze.

"*Sasha*, lemme' hollar at you in private for a minute." Miles escorted Sasha further into the penthouse. He noticed a sunken marble floor and some other extravagant luxuries, but remained focused. "Listen . . . my friend comes with me on big money transactions. She's not an average woman. So please . . . *please* mind your manners around her."

"But I told you, I only do—"

"So we can go to another room. Whatever. Just give the woman some respect, *huh*?" Miles patted Sasha on the shoulder and stepped past him. Sasha offered a salty smile to Charmaine standing there, attaché case in hand. "Nice place you got here. How long you stayin' at the hotel?"

"I live here," Sasha said. "It's convenient."

"*And expensive*," guessed Miles, trying to forget their earlier telephone duel.

"It's the good life . . . Whaddaya want from me." Sasha and Miles sat at a table by the window. There was a view of the Manhattan skyline to accommodate the moment.

Out of the blue, Sasha said, "So," as if to get to the matter at hand.

"You have the money?"

"I have five hundred. It's in large bills, as usual."

"Good. When would I get the rest?"

"Same as before. Three, maybe four days."

"I'm gonna need half the money. Six hundred sixty-six thousand."

"I only have five."

"You know and *I know* you're lying. You told me long ago that you keep a million liquid for special occasions. What? You get anmesia all of a sudden?"

Sasha fumed and said, "Let me see African Queen."

Miles looked toward Charmaine across the penthouse floor. She realized his signal and came over with the attaché case. Miles took it, placed it on the table and spun it in front of Sasha. Sasha ignored that Charmaine was standing there, his mind locked on the most important thing. He released the snaps and flipped open the attaché.

"*Incredible.* Absolutely . . . in-*credible*." Sasha took out the loupe, that eyepiece which jewelers use to examine precious stones.

"Sasha, let's not make a big affair out of this. That's your diamond. Now let's finish up."

Sasha looked up at Miles, his mood one of possession instead of want or desire. Charmaine sensed apprehension and unzipped her FILA top. She had a black knit top that hugged her shape, but the attention was drawn to the pistol in her shoulder holster. Sasha didn't have any doubt she knew how to use it.

"Yes," Sasha said. "Let's finish up."

* * *

The wait in apartment 1C was both sweet and sour. Iris was so cute that Elvis couldn't take his eyes off of her. She almost seemed to tease him the way she catered to them, making eggs and bacon and toast, and batting her eyes as if shopping her own jewels in front of the visitors. Elvis imagined what she'd be like in bed underneath him. It was the first time he'd thought about another woman since Melanie came along.

While Elvis gawked at Iris, Chanté sat on a high chair next to the door. She had a stack of magazines such as *Essence*, *Honey* and *Today's Black Woman* to keep her busy. Every so often she'd look up to peek at Elvis with his tongue virtually hanging out of his mouth, or at Sonny, who kept changing the T.V. channel. *Damn that remote control and Sonny too, with his nervous ass.* She dared Sonny to gaze at her as Elvis was at Iris.

At minutes to 8, Chanté answered the phone. Then she said, "Time to go."

Sonny didn't know whether to expect Miles to pop up at the door or if Rose would stop by to confirm that the deal was done. It made him edgy, worried and restless all at once. And now that the phone rang, with Chanté being vague about where they were going, things didn't seem to be kosher. Did Miles get the money? Was there a problem? Was this it? Was Rose gonna feed Sonny and Elvis to Buck and Nitro?

Sonny braced himself as Chanté opened the door to 1C. Miles was standing there just over the threshold.

"Man you had me worried *shit*. How'd it go?"

"Let's go. We'll talk in the car. Come *on* Elvis," Miles said, pulling Elvis away from trying to cop a phone number from Iris.

When Miles gave a twenty-dollar tip to the homeless man for watching the Mercedes outside of Rose's crib, Sonny just knew they'd gotten paid. He couldn't wait to jump in the car and get movin' so that he could count *his*. And the instant the doors shut, Sonny asked, "What happened?" Miles pulled away from the curb and headed to the end of Manhattan

Avenue, before he cut a right turn and circled around to 125th street. Homebound.

"Under the seat," Miles said. Sonny's hand shot between his legs and felt around. There was a brown paper bag with rolls of money bound rubber bands.

"How much is here?"

"Count it if you want. There's a hundred grand there. Break up the rolls into three equal parts."

As Sonny pieced apart the rolls he asked, "Why only a hundred?"

"I talked Sasha into taking a third instead of half. I explained that because of complications we had to pay off a third party. I lied and said it would keep the police off of us. He was scared shit about the police, so we shook on the deal."

"Shit. That's . . . you mean the three of us gotta split up the third?"

"You got it."

"So why we only got a hundred?"

"The man only had six hundred in cash to give me. I had to give Rose five hundred just to make *him* happy to get you two out of there, and that's what's left."

"I thought Rose only wanted a third?"

"He does. I owe 'em a hundred. We agreed he'd take just six when all is said and done."

"And what about ours?"

"After our partners get paid? We end up with a little more than two hundred and forty each."

"We're still fuckin' rich Sonny. What's the difference," said Elvis.

"Some of us have plans dog. Some of us don't sniff up half the money we make or blow it on—"

"SONNY!" Miles cut him off. Not wanting Sonny to reveal what Miles told him on their way to the city, how Elvis picked up a bartender on a one-night-stand deal. How that same chick was probably laying waiting for a sugar daddy to step in and sweep her off her feet. "The bottom line is we pick up the rest of the cash tomorrow. In full. We give Rose his hundred."

"Extortion money," said Elvis.

"*Whatever*. As soon as I get this dough, I'm out of the jewelry game. For *good*." Miles let those words marinate. Then he said, "'Nother thing, we gotta put some money together for Gus."

Sonny asked, "How much," as if the dollars were being pulled from out of his pockets before they got there.

"At least twenty. Elvis you don't know Gus like we did, so if you don't—"

"If? Come on, dog. Count me in. Without Gus we wouldn't even *have* this money."

"Solid. That'll be enough to bury him like I want. Plus get his pops a good lawyer."

CHAPTER SEVENTEEN

"Miles! Miles! It's the phone for you. Some attorney named Levy. Says he wants to talk to you about a Mr. Chambers."

"Alright, Mom," Miles said, feeling the impression she was trying to make. They were in a two-family house now, a townhouse divided, with its entrances sharing a single porch. Living to the left of his mother gave Miles the convenience of her being near. However it was a year ago this month that Miles and Bambi agreed to this on one condition: that she not intrude on their relationship. None of that *just stopping by*. No coming over to do cooking (except maybe for special occasions) or cleaning, both of which Bambi intended to handle for "her man." If they happened to have an argument, and if Mom happened to "overhear" the spat, there was to be no meddling. They were young and in love. Arguments would be expected, to an end which would ultimately have them understanding one another even more.

Bambi was away this afternoon. Downtown at The Hit Factory, doing background vocals for Joe's latest album. She'd been working on her demo for months now, and once a popular R&B producer got wind of her talent, he began utilizing her for background vocals on the albums of a few acts whose work he mixed and remixed. There was talk of going on tours with one or two of these artists, however, Miles hadn't yet agreed with the idea.

Since Bambi was away, as usual, Mrs. Green would stop by to be a mother to her son. Miles allowed this but asked her to please leave things as she found them. One woman's touch was enough. Anything more would be a signal, causing complications with his wife-to-be.

One year. A year during which the biggest changes in Miles's life took place.

"I'll take the call up here!" Miles shouted from upstairs where he was putting on finishing touches to his suit. This was also the 1st anniversary of Gus's death. Sonny, Miles, and Elvis vowed to visit his grave each year in his memory. Miles still had 45 minutes before the gathering. "Miles Green speaking," he said, was the way he answered the phone these days. Direct and to the point.

"Yes, Mr. Green, this is Joel Levy. You asked that I call you if in fact there was good news concerning Mr. Chambers's case."

"Right. I remember."

"Well the twenty-two fifty motion has been found in our favor and the civil court has ordered the district court judge to re-hear the case."

Miles was fiddling with his tie, wanting Sonny and Elvis to respect the details of a progressive black man who did better with his money then they had with theirs.

"Mr. Levy, can't you tell me the bottom line? I'm not familiar with all the legal terms."

"What this means is that I got the case reopened. I'm getting Mr. Chambers a new trial."

"Fantastic!" Miles said, not entirely focused on the full meaning of this latest development.

"Is it possible that you'll be able to meet with me to discuss the strategy and how I'd like to proceed?"

"Strategy? Hey, I'm no lawyer sir. I'm not even so much knowledgeable about the case. I can't be of help—"

"Well," Mr. Levy said, coming to his point. Finally.

"There is the matter of payment."

"*Payment?* We gave you twenty grand."

"Sure. Sure, I realize that. However taking this case to

trial is another story altogether. What you paid me for was the post conviction motions. The trial and court proceedings however require many man hours and—"

"WOW. You lawyers are somethin' else. You'd think that a man's liberty was more important than these . . . *fees*." Miles was actually thinking "extortion monies."

"Can I call you back about this? I'm in kind of a hurry right now."

"Sure. I'd be glad to hear from you."

"Thank you," Miles said. He hung up and then said, *"I'm sure you would."*

Miles kissed his mother and said, "Mom I gotta run. But please, *please* don't do nothin' crazy in here. We agreed."

"Oh, don't be silly, Miles," she said, kissing her one and only on the forehead and running her hand over his face. Miles imagined how he'd have to come home in time to change things back to normal (again) so that Bambi wouldn't feel his mom's presence.

Miles jumped on the Bronx River Parkway, anticipating the three exits he'd have to drive, thinking about Gus and his father. Miles didn't know the elder Chambers except for what he'd seen from a distance on the day of the funeral.

The state's Department of Corrections had permitted Gus's father to attend the funeral so long as various authorities and expenses were paid for. Armed prison guards, 4 city police officers, 2 US Marshals, etcetera, etcetera, etcetera. The bill came to $10, 000, but it was all for their friend Gus. It was the least they could do seeing as how Gus wouldn't be alive to enjoy his piece of the pie. Miles recalled how they brought Mr. Chambers in his green jumpsuit, handcuffed and shackled. It was a small funeral with few witnesses. Mostly friends from around Gus's neighborhood, folks that Miles had bussed to the cemetery. Miles, Sonny and Elvis had to watch the funeral through binoculars, concerned that detectives would be present in search of Gus's friends—those who might've been involved with a certain car accident, a certain jewelry heist, on a certain expressway in Long Island.

At the time, while they watched the proceedings from afar, the three entertained themselves by discussing how they could rain down on the cops who held Gus's pop in custody. They were already skilled at ambushes, for the most part anyhow, and taking out 6 armed officers couldn't be any different. The element of surprise . . . that always made the difference between success and failure in a military coup.

SonnyMiles was positioned closest to the Galleria's main entrance, although there were five such main entrances. Depending on whose perspective, whether it was Macy's on one corner, J.C. Penney on another, or the two other department stores which all together served as anchors for the 4-level mega mall, there were any number of entrances to be considered exclusive. But SonnyMiles, the clothing store which Sonny Stewart operated, was near the entrance where taxis and buses pulled up to drop off passengers. This was the entrance with the huge waiting area, the newsstand and where Santa Claus hung out to ring his bell for donations each year for three weeks.

The location of the store, coupled with the comings and goings of nearly a hundred thousand shoppers a week, lent assurance to an already booming business. The fact that SonnyMiles carried all of the top urban designers just added icing to an already delicious cake. There was an indefinable chemistry between what was the "in" thing to wear and the impulse that burned into the consciousness of tots to adults who were influenced (somehow) in keeping up with the Jones's.

SonnyMiles grossed $400,000 in sales by the end of their second quarter in business. The store grossed $500,000 in the 3rd quarter, and $880,000 in their biggest quarter to date. The average profit margin was 25% to 30%. Both Miles, the absentee owner who received quarterly checks, and Sonny, the hands-on operator of the store, were winning.

"Aren't *you* the pimp today," Dori said, noticing Sonny fixing his tie, all geared up for the meet at the cemetery.

Sonny smirked. "You just make sure to watch my money while I'm gone. This shouldn't take more than an hour." Dori came over to help Sonny with his tie.

"Anything for you, daddy."

"You know you ain't supposed to call me that in the store woman."

"I know. I just can't help myself." Dori reached down and fondled Sonny below the waist. "I can help *you* though."

"Come on," Sonny said after sucking his teeth. "You know I got an important engagement."

"I know. But you're stressed, daddy. Lemme relax you." Dori's hand was already inside of his fly.

"Well shit, I can't leave with my joint all blown up like a flag pole," Sonny said. "Who's workin' the registers?"

"Marcy and Jorinda. Don't worry, I trust 'em." Dori was good at this, at satisfying Sonny on a whim. It was convenient for him. Not only did she help manage the store, but he could get hit off now and again, whenever he or she felt horny. And no, he still didn't love that ho. While Dori busied herself Sonny reached over to lock the office door and leaned back with his ass resting against his desk: Dori sounded like a cat lapping at a bowl of milk; just another stimulating thought as Sonny watched the 4 monitors, the video surveillance exchanging images of various areas throughout the store. He also looked at his Rolex watch, telling himself ten more minutes wouldn't hurt.

Miles was standing alone, his eyes going in and out of focus, probably creating impressions on his mind. Those words chiseled on Gus's gravestone. "HE LIVED AND DIED FOR OTHERS."

Miles knew that message so well. It haunted him on occasion. He forgot about it at others. It was either one way or the other. But never did Miles forget about his buddy Gus. He was a soldier and a friend. Even if he wasn't faithful to the Corps, he was faithful to Miles. And Elvis was right when he made that statement the day after Gus died. "*Without Gus we wouldn't even have this money.*"

"Sorry I'm late," said Sonny. His approach not even rattling Miles, not even disturbing the state he was in. "Traffic on the Bronx River." Sonny stood by Miles now, attempting to settle in on the silence that he interrupted.

Miles turned to look at Sonny. What he immediately noticed was a man who was a bit too relaxed, with lipstick on his collar. *Yeah, sure. Traffic.* Miles would've labeled Sonny a dysfunctional sex fiend at that very instant, but for the mood he'd worked up. Instead, Miles simply turned back to Gus and the two stood quiet for a while.

"You think we did the right thing?" Miles eventually asked, breaking the silence.

"What about?" asked Sonny, happy to hear Miles say something. Anything.

"The Yukon. You think we did the right thing burying him in the Yukon?"

"Hard to say. *Crazy*? Of course. But I believe like you, that Gus would've wanted that. He loved that truck."

"Yeah, but spiritually . . . *spiritually* did we do the right thing."

"Who can say, Miles. Really. Who says what's right and wrong anymore? I mean, if you were God Almighty, would *you* allow that shit that happened with the World Trade Center? Would you allow all those people to die? All those children to go through life without mothers or fathers?"

"You know, now that you mention it, the *way* you mention it, that would be some shit, wouldn't it? To be GOD, sittin' up there in the clouds, or wherever he is, watchin' those planes on their way to the buildings . . . Just sittin' there tellin' himself, okay! *Here goes*! And then, *BOOM*. When that's done he says let's do it again. And the 2nd plane hits. What kind of excuse does God give when people pray or when folks ask why?" Miles lowered his head, as if he was sharing the discussion with Gus as well. "Ain't like God's gonna give excuses: *oh, sorry. I missed that one. Had to take a leak.* Or, *I was busy bonin' Mother Nature.*" Sonny, always with sex on the brain.

"Makes you wonder, huh? Makes you wonder if there *is* a

God. Or if we're all out here lyin' to ourselves. If we're all out here fakin' it, just playin' life by ear." Miles wagged his head ever slightly.

"All of us pickin' a book to follow. To guide us."

"Now that we're speakin' about it, the Yukon I mean, I feel better now. *Sure* we did the right thing. The Egyptians buried King Tut with all that gold so why can't we bury Gus in his truck. His own personal casket."

"Hmmm. I know one thing. The look on his father's face when they lowered the whole truck in the earth? I'd love to have a photo of *that*." Sonny almost chuckled.

Miles smiled. "I guess Elvis took an L on us. Forgot the pact we made."

"I don't know how he could forget. I spoke to him last night."

"He got a phone number now?"

"No Miles. Of course not. I paged him."

"I thought his pager was cut off."

"Me too. But I tried it after I closed the store yesterday. He actually returned my call."

"Where's he livin' now?"

"Believe it or not? He's still at the Ramada Hotel."

"Get the fuck out of here! He's been there all this time? A whole year?" Miles asked.

"Dude . . . he had money just like you and me. Only we did things with ours. He blew his. Dude probably gets room service six times a day, maid service, all that. Plus he's doin' coke with his girl more'n you and I drink water."

"A fuckin' shame," Miles said.

"Got that right," Sonny agreed.

"I guess he'll go back to pushin' guns."

"I guess. You get the check from 3rd quarter?"

"Yeah, I got it. Oh shit. That reminds me. I got a call today. Remember that lawyer we hired for Gus's father?"

"Mmmhmm."

"He called today. Just before I left. Said he got the case reopened. Said he could get a new trial."

"Oh damn. There *is* a God," Sonny said facetiously.

"But there's more. He needs to be paid to take it to trial. Something about man-hours and motions-n-stuff."

"Man. Mo' money, mo' problems, huh? It seems like ever since we got money there's always somethin' to spend it on."

"So what you wanna do?"

Sonny thought about it, sucked his teeth, then said, "Fuck it. It was a good Christmas anyway." Sonny turned to Gus and did a bow. "Merry Christmas Gus. We gonna look out for pops."

Miles smiled, thinking maybe there *was* somethin' in Sonny's head and heart besides sex and money.

CHAPTER EIGHTEEN

Barry Davidson had produced songs and albums for some of the biggest and most renowned names in black music. All told, after twenty-five years of making music, he had been responsible for and credited for more than 30 million albums sold, 42 top twenty hits, 31 that reached top ten, and 17 that went to number one. Eight of his songs have been number one hits on *Billboard*'s top ten pop list. All of this success was a mere mustard seed when weighed beside Quincy Jones or R. Kelly, but these were significant accomplishments nonetheless.

"Bambi, I'm gonna need you to sing the hook again." Barry was speaking into a miniature microphone while depressing a red button. "And put a little more stomach in it this time. Remember your consonants too." Barry was looking out from his electronic kingdom behind a wall of glass that kept two divisions, (the studio and the control room) as separate and isolated entities.

Bambi was on the sound booth side of the glass, although this was far bigger than what the term *booth* denoted. She stood on a polished wood floor that shined so much it seemed wet. The lighting had a medium wattage glare, which allowed for a mellow mood. Even if it was a bright winter's day outside, studio 255 took on the warm and intimate atmosphere of a jazz club. Gray sponge blocks covered the walls and ceilings to keep that snug insulation which all recording studios are known for.

"Okay, Barry. Let's do it."

The song's flute and bells ascended into a captivating opening. Bambi stood behind a microphone with headphones on and her hands pressing them closer to her ears. Her foot pretended to tap the floor, keeping time with the song's melody. When the lead vocal was done, it was Bambi's turn.

"EVER SINCE there was a you, there was a me ... EVER SINCE. We said that we were meant to be . . ."

Bambi stopped the progress this time, holding one hand up to Barry and the other to her stomach.

"You alright, babe?" Barry asked through the mic.

Bambi bent over some and winced.

"Oh, *God*," exclaimed Barry.

Stanley, the engineer who worked the soundboards, jumped up from his seat and took aggressive steps though the two doors that separated the rooms.

"Bambi, what's up? You need water?"

"I think I'm gonna be sick," she blurted.

When Miles arrived at The Hit Factory to pick up Bambi he was shocked to hear the news. He raced back downstairs to the car and took off for Mt. Sinai Hospital, where Bambi had been taken by ambulance. At the hospital they wouldn't let Miles in; he wasn't family, fiancé or not. But this was just an inconvenience to Miles. It had been a while since he had to think contemptuously or deceitfully; since he had to adopt a criminal mind. Now that love was on the line, it was no contest. He circled the hospital, investigated its many doors, windows and garages. A fence stood tall around a trash compactor in a rear driveway. There was a gate on the side where trucks might come to empty the compactor, however the opposite end of the compactor was where custodians emptied garbage. There was no gate there. Nothing to stop Miles from entering an open door once he scaled the fence itself. Once inside, Miles did the little bit it took to get hold

of a custodial uniform and he was home free. The receptionist in the lobby revealed Bambi's room number when Miles
initially approached the hospital, so he took the service elevator to the third floor and found 341.

There was still some daylight that brightened the room
when Miles entered, enabling him to see clearly. Bambi was
hooked up to an intravenous needle feeding her insulin and
a sensor was attached to a finger relaying her vital signs to
an electrocardiograph machine nearby. Maybe it was the
sudden draft that made her open her eyes.

"Miles," she muttered.

"Baby," Miles replied in half-a-voice. "Jesus, they got
you all wired up. What happened?"

"I . . . what are you wearing Miles?" Bambi's voice was
weaker than usual. Perhaps relaxed.

"I had to sneak in. They wouldn't let me see you, only
immediate family."

"Miles."

"What up, boo?"

"I'm pregnant."

"Preg . . . you mean as in baby? You and me?"

"*Whoa* lover. Don't fall out on me now."

"I'm not, I guess . . ." Miles caught his breath and took a
sec to swallow. "I'm just a little overwhelmed. Did they say
what it is? Boy or girl?"

"No *silly*. They can't tell us that *now*." Bambi rolled her
eyes at Miles's naivety.

"Well, shit, I don't know. This is my first time."

"*I'm* the one having the baby."

"Well then it's *your* first time. Yours . . . mine . . . who
cares! We're havin' a baby!" Miles didn't care to contain himself anymore. He didn't care *who* knew he snuck in. Miles
huddled over Bambi, hugging her.

"You mean you're happy? You don't mind?"

"Happy? Do I mind? Girl, I'm the happiest man in the
world right now. I'm so happy I could climb a mountain. I
could fuckin' *fly*!"

Bambi smiled. She said, "Miles our baby is gonna be

beautiful. You and me mixed together. Your eyes, my cheeks.
Your brain, my hair . . ."

"Yeah. Picture that, one baby, with all our talents, our
hopes and dreams and passions." Miles suddenly felt horny,
kissing all over Bambi and climbing halfway onto the hospital bed as he did.

"*Oh*." A nurse sighed as she entered the room. "Sorry," she
whispered, not wanting to be rude as she tiptoed backwards
out of the door. But Bambi and Miles never noticed her.

Elvis lived for the day, the hour and the minute. He craved
those thrills; those feel-good instances that cared everything
about now and absolutely nothing about tomorrow. He and
Melanie did things this way for the entire year following his
big payoff. The folks at the Ramada treated them like roy-
alty; their best customers. Their money was king. Their lifestyle seemed endless. And their passion for bigger, for better,
and for more was insatiable.

The extended stay at the hotel wasn't the original plan.
They were a day from moving into their own Midtown Manhattan penthouse, but the landlord and co-op board turned
Melanie down for poor credit. So this was the way it's been
ever since. Every so often the two went on a trip; a riverboat
casino trip, Atlantic City and a 7-day cruise to the Virgin Is-
lands. Each of those trips had them spend $10,000 whether it
was for gambling, souvenirs or cheap thrills. Then, of course,
there were all the luxuries they demanded; wouldn't live
without them.

Next to the trips, Elvis and Melanie became well-known
on the club scene. They frequented the hottest dance clubs,
and they created a huge fever amongst a small group of post-
teens who followed them and copied their lifestyle. They
called themselves the "Inner Circle," always moving as one
on weekends, often lounging back at the penthouse up at the
Ramada. All the while drugs were in fashion, from beefed
up stogies of marijuana, to intensely potent cocaine, to ecstasy, they did it all.

"Elvis, there's a man at the door says he needs to talk to you." Becky was standing there at the bedroom door wearing a long black t-shirt that was ripped here and there for her golden-pink skin to peek through. The shirt wasn't ripped so much that the bold word "TOY" couldn't be read across the front. Elvis thought about the message Becky relayed and was quickly unhappy that he had to get up.

"He didn't see you like *that* did he?"

"*Course*! It's not as if he can see I don't have panties on." Becky wore a devious smile. Elvis took a pillow and tossed it at Becky, intentionally missing her. But she'd run and shut the door behind her anyway.

"Okay guys. You gotta let up. I gotta see Rocky."

"Come on Elvis," sighed Skyler stretched out on one side of his body, still with her hands holding him tight.

Meanwhile Melanie was slurping away while trying to speak at the same time. "Do you have to go?" Elvis took both their chins in his hands and said, "If it wasn't important I'm sure he wouldn't be up here. Now lemme' up. Keep yourselves busy till I get back." Elvis rose from his nest of fantasies-come-true and wrapped his red silk smoking jacket around his naked body. Melanie and Skyler shrugged and quickly obeyed as Elvis left the room.

From his quiet threesome, Elvis entered the living room where soft jazz was playing in the atmosphere. Becky sat there on the couch, with her one bare limb exposed and folded up on the arm. Her golden ponytail draped over the back of the couch. Joanne was on the floor with Alexis, both of them with their long brunette and black hair spread about their collars, necks and shoulders. Joanne was cheekier than Alexis. Alexis had the sharper definitions along her nose and jaw line. Joanne wore a blue cut-off tee, her navel exposed over white short-shorts. Alexis wore a black halter-top and black thong to go with her hair. Her tan was broadcast real nice against what little clothing she had on. Elvis could hear the other girls in the other bedroom.

"Company. Cover up *something*, damn."

Alexis muted the program the three were watching on "E."

"It's only Rocky dude. It's not like he hasn't seen us like this before."

"Yeah, but." Elvis pleaded with his arms out. Now Becky threw a pillow at Elvis. "You all are gonna be the death of me."

Elvis pulled open the door and without seeing him first he said, "Come in Rocky."

"That's okay Elvis. This is gonna be quick. I just had to ask you to take it easy on the room service." Rocky almost whispered, not wanting to be overheard.

"Take it easy? I don't get it. Are we like a burden all of a sudden?"

"I thought you'd have questions." Rocky took out a folded computer read-out. "This is your bill this month."

Elvis looked at it. $3,100. "Okay. *So*? I've done triple *this* in a month."

"I know. That's what worries me. You haven't paid up on *last* month's bill yet. If you add the rent for this month, last month . . . we're talkin' well over ten big ones."

"You gotta be kiddin' me, Rocky. I've spent well over a hundred gees here. I pay real good."

"*Real* good," Rocky affirmed.

"I mean, what? Alexis didn't hit you off good enough last week? Is *that* what this is about?

Rocky adjusted his hotel blazer, a bit uncomfortable at the shift in subjects.

"Oh, she *did*. Absolutely she hit me off. But it's the higher-ups I gotta answer to Elvis if . . ."

"If what?" Elvis put his hands on his hips. He had raised his voice as well. Rocky reached past him to pull the pent-house door shut.

"Listen Elvis. I'm the last person who wants to stand here and question you. But I'm the first person who's gotta come up with the answers."

"I'll tell you what." Elvis stepped up to Rocky and fixed his collar that didn't need fixing, and dusted off his shoulders which didn't need dusting. "I'll have the bill paid off in full by the end of the week. How's that?"

"Oh shit, well, hell?" Rocky took the read-out and ripped it in shreds. "Ain't shit to worry about."

"Thank you. Sure you don't wanna come in for a little spin-the-bottle, blow-the-hotel manager?"

"Uh . . . no . . . no, I . . . I can't. The wife and I are goin' out to a play tonight."

"Sure? I got Adele in here, the one who can stand on her head and do a split. Or Skyler . . . remember her? She's the one you and me did together."

"Ohhhh, I *definitely* remember her. But, really, I can't." Rocky, Mr. Responsibility.

"Okay. Your loss."

"Maybe a rain check?"

"Sure. Tell the wife I said hi. And get that room service up here!"

Rocky was already at the elevator. Saluting.

"Yes sir."

"Who's the king?"

"You are, Elvis."

"Who?"

"You! Elvis is king!"

"Good. Now be a *good* hotel manager and fly away." Elvis went back into the penthouse. "Whadda you lookin' at," he said, catching all three swinging their heads back towards E. "I think we need to get somethin' straight around here." Elvis folded his arms and had his voice raised. "BECKY, get all the girls out here. NOW!" Elvis, the tyrant. He went to push open his bedroom door. "Okay, the lickin' is over. Get out here. NOW!"

As Melanie and Skyler scrambled off of each other and off of the bed, Elvis strolled over to the night table. He picked up the plate with the rolled-up hundred-dollar bill and numerous lines of cocaine. With the makeshift straw, Elvis snorted up two of the lines and whipped his head in a frenzy afterwards.

He went out to the living room, creating a hush among the eight women in his audience.

"Okay. I'm startin' to sense a little doubt around here. Like somebody, ANYBODY has the balls to doubt the

KING. I'm the FUCKING KING! The motherfuckin' *greatest*. Who's the greatest?"

"You are," they said in a broken chorus.

"No-No-No-No-No-Noooo . . . that shit ain't *believable*. I *said*, WHO IS THE GREATEST?"

"YOU ARE!" they chanted.

"And who's the king?"

"YOU ARE!!"

"Good. Now we start to prove it. Wanda-Ling you first." Elvis curled his finger at the only oriental in his harem. She, with the long black hair down her back, pretty eyes and small-pursed lips, shimmied over willingly.

"Good, good. Obedience. That's what the fuck I respect. Now show everybody why Elvis is king." Elvis pulled open his robe and stood with his legs parted and hands on his hips. Elvis, as Superman.

Wanda-Ling put her hands gently on Elvis' hips and knelt to the plush white carpet. Adele, Becky, Skyler, Melanie, Joanne, Alexis and Cathy stood there in various colors of light clothing, watching their friend service the king.

"Adele, you might as well come on over and help Wanda-Ling. And the rest of you just get naked. Take it all off."

"Elvis, you know we all love you. You don't have to . . ." Melanie's subtle protest quickly aggravated Elvis.

"I don't have to what?"

"To talk to us this way."

"Oh. So now Melanie wants to tell me what to do and what *not* to do, huh."

"No, I . . ."

"Zip it. You got me fucked up. Matter fact, Alexis go get a pitcher of water. Becky help her. *Do it!*" The girls were all naked nymphs now, two of them rushing off to handle the task.

"Melanie lay down on the carpet."

"Elvis, please don't . . ." Melanie pleaded.

"Melanie, I swear, you don't want me to get upset. Now get the fuck on the floor!" Melanie had some apprehension, but she did as she was told. The others came back with the water.

"Okay. I don't know what y'all are waitin' for. Drink! You know the drill."

After Alexis and Becky drank 2 glasses of water each, Elvis had them stand over Melanie, one positioned over her face and neck, the other over her pelvis and hips.

"Good. Now the rest of you, that is . . . except for Wanda-Ling and Adele, count to ten. You know how this works. No pee by ten, both of you drink two more glasses. I want Melanie to look, smell and feel like a urinal. Start countin'!"

Melanie laid there, eyes closed with tears, knowing she should've kept her mouth shut, and that Elvis got beside himself when he's coked up.

CHAPTER NINETEEN

Carnegie Hall was abuzz with glamour tonight. The women were dazzling in high textured or luxurious fabric gowns, high waisted narrow skirts and slinky, sequin tube dresses. The men were fine and dandy in soft, supple cashmere, wool, and high-thread cotton single and double-breasted suits. Some of the older men seemed to be caught in unbearable tightness, with their style of dress as well as with their attitudes, while most of the 30-somethings went for simplicity.

The Paris Opera Ballet was in full motion on stage, its dancers dressed down in shades of blue and white, while the music of Chapentier, Rameau, Vivaldi and FatBoy Slim echoed through the gilded hall. The jumbotron screen behind the dancers projected giant semblances, almost like shadows, in a dual live and electronic production. One peak segment of the show had a dancer engaged in a tit-for-tat duel with a larger prerecorded image up on the screen. Another had the star couple in a romantic, fluid heart-stopping blur, the female being whisked into the air, perched in a split upon her partner's shoulders, or spun about in a long-limbed, incandescent demonstration of beauty. The performance casted a luminous spell on an audience that seemed to hold its breath every so often.

Outside on 57th street, the snow had just begun to fall, dusting the rooftops, hoods and trunks of a who's-who of luxury vehicles. Limousines hogged the most space, with their drivers out and about, holding up signs with names printed in bold, yelling out those names of their riders. "FITZGERALD!" "GOLDBURG!" "SHWARTZ!" "RIDEN-HOUR!" The names were either answered, or they weren't as audience members left the hall's entrance, joyful and smiling. Fulfilled with a night of memorable images and sounds.

Inside the lobby, concert attendees wrapped up in their garb, overcoats and belted trenches. Hats and scarves.

"Dah-ling, why don't you go for the car. Erma and I will look for you."

"Yes! I will brave the snow for my beautiful wife and my lovely sister! Off into the wilderness!" Sasha Franco made a dramatic performance out of a quick trek to the garage.

"He's such an *actor,*" said Erma Franco, his sister, who was up in her years and still husbandless.

"The shows get him this way. Sometimes I have to force a sedative down his throat to keep him quiet."

"You know I really haven't said this, but that ring is ab-so-lute-ly gorgeous."

"Oh thank you dah-ling. It sort of comes with a curse you know."

"Really? What is that?"

"My *husband.*"

The two women laughed heartily as they pulled themselves together, sharing opinions about the ballet as they waited for Sasha.

"Your car is here ma'am . . . madame."

"OH! My how polite of Sasha. He sent an escort?"

"Uh, sure ma'am. I'm here to escort you. Mister . . . uh Sar-sha has hired a limousine for the evening."

"*Mmmmm . . .*" Erma sounded like a human siren, excited about the sudden surprise. The escort stepped aside with a slight bow, all decked-out in black, a belted London Fog, a chauffeur's cap and gloves. The sister and wife braced themselves for the inevitable chill and stepped out of Carnegie Hall, onto the sidewalk and into a waiting black limousine. The driver opened the back door and the two were quickly adjusting to the warmth of the vehicle. The driver hurried around to his place behind the wheel.

"I wonder what surprise your brother has in store . . . this seems mighty strange."

"Is this perhaps your birthday Ivana? Maybe an anniversary you forgot?"

"Not at all," she replied, still shaking the chill.

"Oh well. Let's sit back and just enjoy the rest of the night, wherever it takes us."

The driver lowered the window just enough for his voice to be heard. "We're gonna circle round the block. He has a surprise for you." He raised the window up.

"See? Told ya."

"Gee. Maybe I did forget an occasion," Ivana said.

The limo pulled away from in front of the hall, with its crowd of happy ballet-lovers, and it proceeded down 57th street to 6th Avenue. A left turn at the traffic light took the car to Central Park South with its line of horse driven carriages standing out under the dark sky and its falling snow.

Within minutes the limo had cruised across town to the West side where it parked under the 57th street on ramp to the highway.

Ivana was knocking at the separation window when the rear door of the limousine was pulled open. The driver stepped into the car and slumped into the furthest seat of the car.

"Where's my husband!" hollered Ivana, her arms folded and brow wrinkled.

"He won't be with us this evening."

Ivana reached for the doorknob.

"It's no use. That's locked from the panel up front."

Ivana turned in her crouched position.

"Listen you! You let us out of here this minute." Her finger was boldly in her captor's face. He reached out and thrust Ivana back and she fell against the seat, half onto her sister-in-law.

"What! I never! You bastard!" shouted Erma.

"What is the meaning of this?" Ivana demanded.

"The meaning *is* . . . this is a stick up." He took out a gun and set it across his lap. "And you two are my victims. We call y'all vics around the way. So let's cut the chit chat and get with the jewelry."

"Jewelry? Is that what this is about?"

"Basically."

Ivana took off her necklace and proceeded to give it to him. But as she did she lunged at the robber with her grip on his neck. Her fingernails digging.

Erma screamed, horrified by the sudden violence as the two wrestled. A shot sounded. Ivana fell back against the side couch, her head against the polished-wood service bar. Her eyes were enormous in her face, frozen in time. Again Erma screamed. It came to a point where she was letting out a scream with every breath. And the abductor was left with no choice. He pulled the trigger again, silencing the woman and sending her slumped to the leather seat. In the ensuing moments, the rings, earrings, necklaces, watches and purses were stripped from the victims. Nothing but the thud of the limo's door closing and footfalls in the snow were evidences of the death and devastation left behind.

CHAPTER TWENTY

Sasha Franco still had the car running, double-parked outside of Carnegie Hall, while he was looking for his wife and sister. He couldn't figure out where they'd gone. He said he'd be right back and that accounted for all of 9 minutes. Pay the parking fee. Hand in the stub. Wait for the car and drive around. What was the big deal? They couldn't wait?

"Is something wrong sir?" Speaking to Sasha was one of the suited men who worked for Carnegie Hall.

"My wife. My sister. I cannot find them."

"Two women? Did one have a white dress and the other sky blue with white sequins?"

"Uh yes! Yes, that's them."

"Sir, they left with a chauffeur a few moments ago. The car was waiting right out front." Sasha was both relieved but disturbed to hear this.

"Thank you. Thank you very much," he told the man, knowing that when he got home he'd have a bone to pick with Ivana and Erma.

Sasha got outside just in time to stop an officer from ticketing his car. He jumped in and as he drove off he immediately dialed home.

"Bitch," he said into the phone when there wasn't an answer. He wasn't sure if he'd cursed his wife, his sister or the circumstances that had him driving back to his upper eastside town house alone.

* * *

"Miles! You really need to stop it." Bambi was relaxing with her feet up, sitting back in a comfortable leather recliner that Miles recently purchased. She had a towel wrapped around her head of hair, a terry cloth robe hugging her body, keeping her warm, and a pair of rabbit fur booties for her feet. Miles had just brought her a cup of tea, the latest edition of *Today's Black Woman* and the Vicks inhaler, all of it on a tray to her side. Now he had freed one foot and began to massage it.

"Why baby, I thought you *liked* being pampered."

"Yeah, once in a while. But this has been going on for two weeks. Ever since I left the hospital."

"That's just the point, boo. I don't want you to exert yourself. No stress, that's the idea here. I don't want you to have to lift a finger." Miles was steadily massaging Bambi's foot and calf as he spoke.

"But Miles, I know damned well this special treatment ain't gonna hold up. This is only the 1st month of the pregnancy. Ease up lover. Save some of this pamperin' for later."

"I just don't wanna see you back in that hospital. *Any* hospital."

"This is a special news bulletin for the man known as Miles Green . . . I'm gonna be *back* in the hospital Mister. How else would I have our baby?"

Miles was cuddling Bambi's foot now, eventually giving her tender kisses about the heel, the palm of the foot and the toes. It was as if her words weren't sticking anywhere in his mind; nothing could have him waver from treating her like a queen.

"Stop! You're *tickling* me!" Bambi pulled her foot back.

"You never stopped me before when I kissed your feet. Or, uhem, sucked your toes."

"Right. Well you're starting to annoy me with all this attention. Give a girl some space. You bathe me every freakin' day, feed me like I'm a handicap and I'm tired of you readin' to me every other minute. Give-me-a-*break*!" Miles pouted in mock disappointment. "Oh don't gimme that sour puss. You'll be alright."

"I just want the best for you, boo."

Bambi lowered her voice to an intimate level and said, "Come here Miles. Miles I'm gonna be fine. *We're* gonna be fine and the baby's gonna be fine. I just need you to lay off a bit." Bambi kissed his forehead. "I know you want what's best for me, but you're becoming obsessed. This morning I couldn't even go to the bathroom without you wanting to wipe my ass." Miles' expression was proof enough that the morning's acts might've been a bit overdone.

"Sorry, boo. Maybe I'll go over to Mom's for a while." Miles got up looking depressed, like he could do nothing right.

"Miles." Bambi lifted herself to an upright sitting position. Miles strolled off.

"Miles!"

Miles was already at the door, still ignoring her.

"Miles, you turn around *this minute!* Now come over here."

Bambi hated to compete with Mrs. Green for her son's attention. And she wouldn't hear the end of it if his mother found out Miles had been chased out of the house.

"I said, *come over here.*" Bambi's voice turned sultry, her head tilted and her eyes partially narrowed. Miles obediently approached the edge of the recliner and Bambi licked her lips. She didn't need to speak another word. She just parted her legs so that one was on either side of the chair. She pulled the flaps of the terrycloth robe aside exposing her Garden of Eden. Then she eased back and closed her eyes, knowing that this was *never* a burden, only pleasure from out of this world.

Sonny and Dori often had coffee in the morning to discuss the business of the day. They'd discuss deliveries that were expected from the manufacturers, pricing, and if necessary, employee changes. Sonny sometimes picked up *USA Today* and *The Daily News* when he knew there wouldn't be much to talk about. It encouraged him to stay busy instead of being dragged into a conversation that almost always hinted to a deeper relationship. Sonny didn't want that from Dori, even if she never really got the point. He didn't want to have to drive the stake in her heart either. Didn't want to be so direct, not now anyhow. What Dori was good for was spontaneity. That's it. Nothing more, nothing less. Quickies and overnights.

Sonny was thinking all of these things as Dori leafed through the *Daily News*, knowing damn well that she wasn't reading the paper, that she was scheming. That's when she spoke up.

"WOW," she said. "That's really fucked up. A guy took his wife and sister to the ballet and when it was over he went to get the car, but they jumped in a limo."

"So?"

"So? The limo driver robbed 'em, shot 'em up and had sex with their dead bodies."

"Get the fuck outta here."

"Look. It's right here on page three."

Sonny immediately felt bad for the husband in the photo, the man's distress and tears showing. He read beyond the headline: "JEWELER TAKES HIT, WIFE & SIS RAPED."

"This shit is sick," Sonny exclaimed, still somehow envying the cache of priceless diamonds that the thief got away with. Brilliant . . . wicked, but brilliant, thought Sonny as he read about $180,000 in jewels and the scheme of how the thief rented the limo in a phony name and disguise. It made Sonny think back to his days as a diamond thief and how he and his partners would ambush individuals. It had been almost two years since he'd stopped. However, every image was still fresh on his mind like his favorite thick strawberry milkshake. Remembering made Sonny wanna call Miles.

"Be right back," he told Dori. And he took the newspaper with him to the payphone. Miles picked up on the 1st ring.

"What're you, anxious?"

"Who's this?"

"It's me. Sonny, dumbbell. You see the papers? About this jewelry robbery?"

"Nah. What happened?"

"Daily News says some jewelry dude's wife and sister were murdered and raped. Over hundred eighty large."

"People get robbed everyday, Son."

"Yeah, but this shit was fuckin' brilliant. Not the murders or the rape, I mean how they did it. They used a limo and finessed the women into the joint, in front of hundreds of people, and they just drove off."

"Maybe the new jacks took over where *others* left off."

"I was thinkin' the same thing. Either *that* or this was somethin' we—"

"Anyway, I gotta get back to tending to Bambi, she's due soon ya' know."

"I know, trust me, I know . . . for months now you've been bangin' those words in my head."

"Okay godfather. Gotta go."

"Yeah. Be good."

"Trust me, I am."

Sasha Franco's world was virtually destroyed. He had already caught the news on 1010 WINS, but hadn't put 2 and 2 together yet. Not until the phone call did he realize the news he heard was concerning his wife. And what a way to get the news—by phone. When he got word of his wife and sister he became weak. He trembled for a time and his systems inevitably broke down, causing him to collapse to the floor. Fortunately for Sasha, the police detective who called was on point. He had identification to go on. There was a program booklet left in the limo. The folks at Carnegie Hall had info relating to the credit card used in relation to the ticket stubs found in the program booklet. The detective worked feverishly to get the home address, and once he did so within minutes, he himself sped across town to east 92nd street, radioing for an ambulance along the way. Meanwhile, EMS workers broke in the front door to the town house to find Sasha laid out on the floor in the midst of a mild heart attack.

"You were lucky," Detective Wade said when Sasha eventually gained consciousness. Wade had been with the 45th precinct (up in the Bronx) for years, however, he was promoted to assistant chief of detectives and recently accepted the position at the Midtown precinct. This was his 14th and 15th homicide case; his 1st and 2nd at his new job. "Imagine if I hadn't been on the phone with you. There'd be nobody to come to your rescue."

"It was you who called?"

Wade stuck out his hand. "Detective Wade. Midtown." With his other hand he pulled a business card from the shirt pocket under his tweed blazer. "Glad to hear you're better and, er sorry I had to break the bad news about your wife and sister. I would've waited until I met you face to face, but you kept jumping to conclusions."

Sasha said nothing. The pain suddenly returning to his consciousness.

"I'm gonna be brief here, 'cuz I know you'll wanna recuperate. This heart stuff is serious." Wade looked across at the nurse, essentially asking for some privacy. "Do you have any enemies, sir? Any reason why someone would wanna come after you?"

"The jewels, of course. That's what this was about," Sasha said under his breath.

Sasha started to wonder if the detective knew about the jewels since they were stolen. But he answered the question before it was asked.

"We interviewed some folks who were sitting beside you three at the ballet. There were also marks on your wife's neck, wrist and ring finger, impressions which would indicate jewelry was a constant."

"Oh."

"So. About your enemies?"

"Sorry, Detective. I don't think I have enemies. I deal with many customers and salesmen, but no enemies."

"Do you have any idea what your wife's and sister's jewelry was worth?"

"My wife wore a ring that carried over ten carats and a necklace that was rectangle, a long, sort of flowing pendant. Rows and columns of one carat diamond drops."

"And how many carats was that?"

"Ten columns down, fives across. Fifty carats."

"So," Wade asked with his hand steady, keeping notes in his pocket pad. "If you could tally up the value of everything how much would you say?"

"Over one hundred, seventy-five."

"Thousand?"

"Yes. Thousand detective."

Wade let that number sink in, then he said, "One more thing Mister Franco. Where would a diamond robber take such expensive jewelry? Where would he cash it in?"

"I . . . I don't know, detective. Somewhere . . . a pawnshop maybe."

"What about where you work, on Forty-seventh street. Would any of those guys buy stolen goods?"

"Well, they're not *supposed* to." Wade read between the lines and decided to do some more investigating along 47th street. This robbery was too well planned to be spontaneous. Someone knew about Sasha Franco. Someone set him up. And if Wade dug deep enough, he might get to the bottom of this.

"I'll leave you alone for now sir. Please get better. I'd like to find your family's killers."

"Thank you, detective."

Detective Donald Wade was from the old school. It was his experience that the people who did the worst things did them to people who they knew personally or who they knew about. He also factored in hate, revenge or error in his opinion on assaults and killings.

Wade didn't make blind presumptions on the subject. He had a track record of solving these kinds of puzzles. The stripper up in the Bronx who attracted the lethal attention of *her lover's* ex-boyfriend. The college teacher who killed two of his students for fear of exposure to his unethical extra-curricular activities. The drug kingpin that got shot up by his ex-girlfriend up in the Co-op City.

It was all patterned after the same concept: "Know your killer." This was a saying that the boys back at the 45th used time and again. Every time a disgruntled employee, a disturbed boyfriend or an unhappy business partner was dragged into the station, booked and arraigned, it confirmed the formula. "Know your killer."

Wade visited the diamond district once more, this time to do a little more than just snoop around. He had to learn the trade, how most diamonds came from South Africa, controlled by a corporation known as DeBeers, and they filtered through The Syndicate which then turns around to appropriate certain diamond stock to sites, those reputable privately-owned and publicly held corporations, diamond brokerages and workshops. Eventually the legions of salespeople get their hands on them.

There were different grades of diamonds, determined by the color. There were also different shapes. Wade learned abut the "three C's." Color, carats and clarity. One jeweler explained, "Stolen diamonds are often times distinguishable, so sometimes they're broken down into smaller pieces. So when a customer first approaches me, I first ask them if they've got the certificate."

"Certificate?"

"Sure. The American Gem Society certifies pieces once they're created, more or less guaranteeing the weight, grade, etcetera. If someone comes in without that, I'm immediately wary. It could be stolen. I generally ask where the piece came from. I listen closely. If it smells funny I ask if they'd like to leave it with me for further review. If they say no, see this button?" Wade looked behind the counter to where the jeweler pointed. "I press this and the diamond police come. There are plainclothes cops at both ends of the block and all in between. They're all waiting for the next diamond thief to rear his ugly head."

"Can you introduce me to their main guy?"

"It was called the African Queen," the pudgy man with meaty fingers said. He had some sort of accent, but Wade couldn't tell if it was Albanian, Italian, Irish or just another New York idiosyncracy. "The reports said a group of guys ambushed this poor little Jewish guy, then a pack of women on motorcycles came by and took it from *those* thieves by gunpoint. That story is legend around here and it only took place a couple years ago. In fact, there were quite a few diamond heists back then."

"Any leads?" Wade asked.

"Well, that's not really our job. We kinda watch Forty-seventh street and that's it. Nobody steals a diamond from this block and gets away. Not alive, anyways."

The African Queen. That stuck in Wade's head as he searched through *Daily News* microfilm. He found the story and it noted the Nassau County Police Department in Long Island. After more interviews he learned about one of the alleged thieves, a Gus Chambers who died in the L.I.E. ambush. It led Wade back to the Bronx.

"So, just like that," Wade asked the landlord of Gus' South Bronx studio. "Nobody asked any other questions or came for further investigation?"

"No sir. They came, they looked, and they asked questions. I gave it a week before I had the studio cleaned up and sanitized. Smelled horrible down there. Like a seedy motel room," a nice, petite woman said.

"Can I take a look?"

"Detective . . . the studio has been rented for almost 2 years now. There is nothing left of that man."

Wade realized he'd wasted time asking and said, "Thank you."

"Oh, detective."

"Yes, ma'am?"

"I do recall telling the police about a black Mercedes."

"Oh?"

"Sure. My son said that a black Mercedes with a black man and black woman stopped here." Wade thought *black-black-black*.

"He saw them stop in the studio and they left after awhile."

"When was this?"

"Around the time . . . well, after Mister Chambers met his maker."

"Was there any license plate recorded?"

"I don't think so."

"Thanks for your help."

There was no way to trace a black Mercedes without a license plate number. There had to be tens of thousands of them in the Bronx. And it wasn't certain that Mr. Chambers's visitors were from the Bronx in any event.

Wade was left with few options. He decided to take the quick trip to the cemetery where Gus Chambers was buried. Since he was hitting dead ends from the world of the living, he figured he'd work the case from the opposite direction, from the ground up.

The groundskeeper was a little frightening to look at, how his eyebrows darted inward, how his afro was unkempt and how his face was wrinkled outside of his eerily-white eyes. Wade wondered if this guy ever auditioned for a vampire movie.

"Gates is the name, the cemetery is my game," the man said as he shook hands with the detective. The two were stepping into the cemetery office since Wade noticed how Gus Chambers's grave had fresh flowers planted and that it looked well maintained in contrast to others.

"I wonder if you have any records of who might be footing the bill for this plot," Wade asked Gates.

"I never really got into names, but a couple a fellas stop by here, just the other day in fact, on the anniversary of the death. They give me a nice tip and I make sure the gravesite looks good. Some burial that was there," Gates said as he picked through a file cabinet.

"How do you mean?"

"Well for one, the dearly departed was buried in a truck."

"A *truck*?"

"It's what I said. They lowered that man's body behind the steering wheel, in the earth."

"You mean to tell me there's a truck buried in the ground out there?" Wade turned to look outside as if he would see anything different from what he'd already seen.

"Yup. With a Mister . . . here it is . . . A Mister Gus Chambers. Twenty-five he woulda been this year. Even took pictures of the funeral."

Wade looked over the folder. There were two Polaroid photos paper clipped to a maintenance contract.

"I'll be *damned*. They actually buried this guy in a Yukon."

"That's the one," Gates confirmed. "I guess you believe me now."

Wade reviewed the contract. The expense was billed to the SonnyMiles Company with a P.O. Box in the Bronx. The signature below was scribbled. Unreadable.

Wade made notes of the particulars and was given a photocopy of the funeral.

Back in the comfort of his apartment Wade soaked into his couch and ignored his dogs. Both of them sulked there on the carpet, waiting for their provider to call them over and cuddle up on the couch beside him. But Wade wasn't in the mood for that now. This was serious. He was studying his notes. Staring at the funeral snapshot. Telling himself that there was NO WAY anyone in their right mind was gonna throw away a brand new GMC Yukon . . . bury it *in the ground*? Who was Gus Chambers . . . *King Tut*? Wade realized he'd wandered somewhat from Sasha Franco's case to this one, the African Queen theft. But he followed his heart. His heart was telling him that there was a particular pattern between the two. He couldn't pick it out right now. But it was *something* that was pulling at him.

Maybe, if he was lucky, all diamond thieves knew one another. Maybe the ones involved with Gus would tell on the ones who hit Sasha Franco. That's how these things worked. You got caught and then you got desperate and told.

"A fuckin' *Yukon*," Wade said to his dogs. "Can you believe?" Then he signaled the dogs to his side. They jumped up ecstatic as could be, tongues all over the place. Wade, as Mister Softee.

"Information."

"Yes operator. Do you have a number for the SonnyMiles Company?"

"In the Bronx?"

"Sure," Wade answered and waited.

"I have Sunny Farm, Sunny Car Wash, Sun Corps, Sun Day Health. . . ."

"No, none of those."

"I have a SonnyMiles in the White Plains?"

"White Plains Road?"

"No sir. White Plains, New York. At the Galleria."

CHAPTER TWENTY-ONE

Elvis had to calm his ass down. His nerves were rattling like the broken muffler skating under a moving car. And this was to be considered a *good day*. The worst of these unbearable times were the hours immediately following the robbery. He'd never actually shot anyone before, not to mention two women; innocent lambs. When he was through taking jewelry, cash and sex, he trekked quickly through the falling snow, just a few blocks up 57th street to the Ramada. When he got up to the penthouse he directed all of his houseguests to one room and had them stay there until *he* said so. Then he flipped on New York 1, the local cable news station, waiting for any sign of the crime that he only recently pulled off. More insane was how hot he felt. He was sweating until his clothes were dripping and eventually until he wet up the couch. For the next 12 hours he kept the women entrapped in the one bedroom while he sat naked and scared to death in front of the television. By the next day Elvis realized he had little to worry about. There were no police sketches on the news, and the anchors said there were "no leads." None of the newspapers, *The Times, The Post* or *The News*, had any more information than the other. No suspects. By noon, the paranoia wore off and Elvis let the girls out of lock-down.

"We're gonna have a party," he told them.

But they weren't enthusiastic as they would otherwise be.

Over 12 hours locked in the room was like packing eight live trout in a bowl to share whatever resources that were available. The girls were not happy.

"Come on now, fix those sorry faces. You know you're not gonna leave me. The living is too good. The coke is too good. And the sex is out of this—"

"I'm outta here you weird-ass wannabe pimp!" Adele strutted off, purse in hand, comfortable in what little she wore.

"Fuck you. And don't come back, bitch." The penthouse door slammed shut behind Adele. "Now . . . anybody else wanna leave paradise?"

Elvis began peeling off bills, willing the girls over one by one and slipping the money in the waistbands of their panties, under their bras, or (in Wanda-Ling's case), he wet the bills and stuck them to her skin.

"Now that everybody is smiling again, let's get freaky!" Elvis, as Hugh Hefner.

It was three weeks later when Elvis decided to cash in on the jewels. He knew that the local fences wouldn't give him what the catch was worth. What he didn't know was that they'd offer him so little. Thousands? Were they kidding or something? The newspapers said the robbery was worth over $180,000. Not to mention the $600 in cash, or the credit cards which later reaped Elvis $18,000, milked out of various ATM's. And a few large mail order purchases that he liquidated. It was the jewels however that he was certain would turn out as the ultimate payoff.

So his mind was going through erratic changes. His body was chilled and rigid. And his nerves were rattled. Elvis was parked on 47th street; across from a place he'd once followed Miles to, shortly after the robbery at the video shoot. (Elvis recalled that there was a rapper involved, but he couldn't remember his name. *Here today, gone tomorrow.*) The thing that had Elvis so edgy was the idea of this being a foreign territory. He never visited this place before, except from a distance. And he certainly didn't know how to approach these big-Willie establishments. The discomfort was enough to make Elvis think of Miles and how badly he needed him this very minute.

But this was Elvis's lick. Why should he give up a percentage to Miles? Miles didn't dream up the limo-at-the-ballet idea, or stake out Carnegie Hall, looking for the most expensive jewelry on the most vulnerable individuals. That was all Elvis' work. Therefore, Elvis realized, he'd have to continue to go it alone till the very end. Meanwhile, he sat, watched and grew whatever encouragement he could as a stranger would in an unfamiliar environment. Maybe by noontime he'd feel better about this.

Sasha Franco's whole life was about diamonds. Or at least it had been. Diamonds made him a lot of money, they grew him a successful business, but they also made him greedy. And they were the reason why his wife Ivana and dear sister Erma were now dead. The mild heart attack made Sasha re-evaluate his life. He wasn't sure what direction he'd take, but it sure wouldn't be to chase rocks that women died for and which men killed for. Rocks.

Sasha was just clearing out some last minute items from his rental space on 47th when the phone rang. It was a reminder to him that he had to call the phone company to inform them of his shop closing. This would be the very last call he'd take on this phone, in this establishment. After this, Sasha Franco the diamond dealer was through. Retired.

"You're the lucky caller," he answered.

"Mr. Franco?" The call had static, like so many mobile phone calls he'd taken.

"Speaking."

"Sir, this is Detective Wade. Midtown. I tried to reach you at home . . ."

"Yes detective. I'm here only momentarily, actually closing up shop today."

"Oh? For good?"

"Yes. For good," Sasha answered, his eyes connecting with other jewelers in his vicinity, all of them with compassionate expressions in light of their neighbor's terrible experiences.

"I just had a question for you. Small thing really. Have you met anyone, or do you know somebody personally who's black and who owns a late model black Mercedes?" Wade wasn't sure if the words came out right, however he got his point across.

"Detective, I must've had many black clients who drove the Mercedes. I never checked the color of their cars however. I'm sorry."

"Alright. Just a thought."

"Goodbye detective."

"Goodbye—oh! Mister Franco. One other thing. Have you heard of the African Queen diamond?"

Sasha was floored. It was as if all the blood suddenly rushed from his body, leaving him limp and numb. Did the detective know he'd set that up? That he'd broken that stone down into smaller pieces for a three million profit?

"Oh, sure. Everyone in my business knows about African Queen, detective."

"Of course—of course. Well I just wondered if you had an idea where a jewel like that might end up. Or would it be broken down and resold?"

Sasha suddenly had to pee. And he wanted to hurry the call before the detective got to reading his thoughts through the phone.

"I really—Detective, my mind is not in business right now. I've lost my wife and sister. My shop is closed. My health is bad." Sasha had raised his voice over the phone, intending to sound distressed.

"I'm sorry, Mister Franco. Tell you what . . . you call me at *your* convenience. When you're feeling up to it. I won't bother you again."

"Thank you. Goodbye, detective."

Sasha was relieved to get the man off of the phone. He suddenly felt weak and had to hold onto the empty glass showcase to stop from falling.

"You okay Sasha? You need a doctor?" A jeweler from

across the way hurried over to help. Others stood by concerned.

"No, thank you. I'll be fine. I guess I need some water."

Detective Wade was parked in the lot that ran the length of the Galleria Mall when he called Sasha. It was another way of making the most out of every God-given moment. On one hand he was waiting for SonnyMiles to open, and on the other there were those questions that were urging him to be curious, begging to be asked. All this talk about diamonds, diamond robberies, and deaths that went with them. These robberies involved big-money items. Not the type a fence would be caught with. Not the type a pawnshop would handle. Wade couldn't help but to wonder about the mentality of a person, who would take a life, risk a life, for the want of a stone. For the love of money.

He waited until 10am, time enough for the store keepers to get themselves situated. Early enough so as not to interfere with any accumulation of customers and potential commerce.

The Galleria was experiencing that climate which wasn't as thunderous as the holidays, and yet there was that mist of fresh air with hopes for a new year with its new styles, new passions and its thrills.

Wade felt a familiarity inside the mall. The temperature was controlled. There was vibrant, buyer-inspiring music wafting overhead. The window displays were appealing to the mind, with mannequins that smiled, colors that bloomed and the windows themselves creating a crystallized façade for each eye-catching arrangement. Meanwhile, the clothing stores intentionally targeted particular age groups and tastes, even if they had to be so bold in doing so. JUST TEENS. FOR GENTLEMEN ONLY. MOTHER-TO-BE. BABY'S WORLD. EXECUTIVE APPAREL. Not to mention how many of these varieties were owned by the same parent companies. It seemed as though there was nothing original anymore. Everything was a knock-off of everything else.

There were the bookstores, theme stores and music stores

that served as universal attractions, already with their wide-spread popularity. Finally, there was the dining area with its franchises in chicken, beef and fish, and its varieties of American and international cuisines. The kiosk near the entrance showed Wade that SonnyMiles was located in the food court, and it was just as easy to find with the glossy black signage over the storefront, and the bright yellow sun behind superimposed scripting of the outlet name. Wade noticed that the store was twice the size of many other had windows full of name brand urban wear. Even Wade heard of and recognized what the kids were wearing nowadays. How many offenders had he seen dragged into the precinct with baggy this and oversized that. Sometimes it made the front lobby of the station look like a *Vibe Magazine*-sponsored fashion show.

"May I help you, sir?"

"I hope so. I'm looking for the manager, or someone who can help me with a few questions?" Wade made a subtle show of his badge.

"Well, uh, I'm the store manager. Maybe I can be of assistance."

"Actually, I may have the wrong place. I saw this name SonnyMiles printed on a contract at a cemetery in the Bronx."

"A contract?"

"Sure, in other words, the person or company which covers the expenses."

"I see."

"Now." Wade pulled out his notebook. "There was a P.O. box with the name . . . out of the Bronx."

The store manager sucked her teeth, confused, and she said, "Maybe someone . . . hold on. Lemme speak to my boss." She strolled to the back of the store.

Before Dori passed through the doorway to the rear office and storage area, she was already calling Sonny's name. He had been up on a ladder checking the storage code and matching it against a list on his clipboard when she approached.

"What's up," he said, hardly turning his head.

"There's a man, a Detective Wade out front. He has some questions that I can't—*ohh!*"

Sonny suddenly lost his balance on the ladder. The clipboard fell from his hands as he grabbed hold of some shelving. Dori held onto the ladder, reaching up to help keep Sonny stable.

"Shit," Sonny sputtered.

"What's wrong?" Dori asked, petrified that Sonny almost fell.

"What's he want? What'd he ask you?"

"Something about the SonnyMiles name on a contract at a cemetery and a Bronx P.O. Box."

"Fuck." Sonny was already down from the ladder pulling Dori to the doorway. He took a peek out front. "Good. He's still at the front counter. Did you tell him I was here?"

"N . . . no . . . I said I speak to my boss. Sonny, what's going on?"

Sonny had his hands tight on Dori's arms as he said, "Listen to me very carefully. Tell him you tried to reach your boss on the phone, but there was no answer. If he asks, tell him your boss' name is . . . uh . . . Mary. Yeah. You got that? Mary."

"Sonny. You tell me what's going on right now." Sonny kissed Dori's forehead, then he cuddled her cheeks with both hands and kissed her lips. "Do what I told you. We'll talk later. Hold down the fort and stay near the phone." Sonny was leaving through the back door where the store's trash was placed and where large deliveries were made. One of the Galleria's indoor alleyways. Dori stood wagging her head, wincing, with her hands on her hips. What was going on?

"Detective, I'm sorry, I can't get her on the phone."

"Her?" Wade's eyes stretched to look behind Dori.

"Yes. Mary. She's my boss."

"Oh. And who was the man you were speaking to?"

"I don't know what—*Detective!*"

Wade pushed past Dori and invaded the back room. He

glanced quickly at the empty office and instinctively shot towards the back door. "Hey! Come back here!" Wade shouted down the alley. He started off in the direction where a man was running, avoiding heaps of garbage that were piled by the back doors of all the stores. All the while, Wade knew he was onto something.

When Sasha came out of his spell of weakness, dizzied with more conclusions than he cared to entertain, he decided on one more phone call. This one, *he'd* initiate. In the box of items he'd cleared from the back office was a Rolodex. He took it out and found the pager number for Miles.

Miles was playing Daddy. Tank was amusing him, already with the firm grip on his daddy's pinkie finger. Smiling and projecting joy as only newborns could do. Bambi was in the kitchen preparing those miniature bottles of warm milk, trying to make friends with Mrs. Green who had become more and more a frequent visitor once Bambi had the baby. It was a helping hand, which Bambi couldn't turn down, nor could she deny.

When the cellphone went off, vibrating on Miles' hip, he was laying on the bed play fighting with Tank, taking his baby boy's hand and helping him to make a fist and then to land a jab, a hook and an uppercut to his father's chin. Miles made all the sound effects of the punches and also of the victim, and then pretended to be knocked out cold. Tank climbed onto his daddy's face to see if he was really dead, and Miles was playing his part real good until the interruption.

"Boo!" Miles said, making Tank smile. Then he looked at the digitized screen of his cellphone. "Whoa!" Miles said, dragging the word as if he wanted his horse to slow to a stop. He hadn't seen *this* phone number on his screen since two years earlier. It was a familiar number, but not really. It took a moment to digest it. To reconnect some signals and cross wires in his brain for a positive identification to come to light.

It wasn't until Miles punched the redial option on his telephone that he realized who called. He was apprehensive at first. But his curiosity picked at him. He followed through with the call anyhow, curious about the "911" on his screen.

"It was you, *wasn't* it," Sasha answered the call with not so much as a hello. He just pressed charges right off the bat. "The police have been onto you for some time now. They know about the jewelry, the black Mercedes, all of it. I just have one question: Why did you have to *kill* them? Why did you have to *rape* them?"

Miles was listening but he *wasn't* listening, too shocked at the "*police being onto him.*" When Miles eventually came around to asking what the hell Sasha was talking about, the connection went dead. Miles tried to call back but there was no answer. Fear and worry overcame him. Then the phone rang.

"It's me, Sonny . . . The cops came by the store today. We gotta talk. We gotta get together *now.*"

"Yeah I know. The park . . . Where we had the picnic?"

"Twenty minutes."

"You got it."

CHAPTER TWENTY-TWO

Elvis was buzzed into the largest of the establishments in the diamond district, the storefront he'd seen Miles enter two years earlier. He was thrown off by how open the venue was, just like a flea market, with stalls, booths, kiosks and numerous glass-enclosed showcases filled with displays and miniature trees of diamonds. Every arrangement was a spectacle. Elvis also quickly caught on to the video surveillance overhead. But that wasn't a hindrance since he was never convicted of a crime; there'd be no data or likeness of Elvis by which to match any video footage with; no police drawings (so far as he knew) that would raise a red flag. And secondly, Elvis came to conduct a business transaction, not to rob or steal. At least, not now.

As Elvis meandered ahead, an older unshaven man pushed past him, upset about something and leaving through the venue's entrance. Elvis shrugged it off, focused on bigger things.

"Excuse me, it says here that you buy jewelry."

"Yes we do. Need an estimate?"

Ira Goldright couldn't believe his eyes, or the irony in the timing. This was one of the most beautiful pieces of jewelry he'd ever seen. It was a diamond necklace, rectangular in shape like a stick of Doublemint gum, flowing vertically for about 2 inches, with half as much width. Its diamonds amounted to a total of 50 one-carat drops, each one as symmetrical as the bead of a raindrop, only sparkling like a tiny star. This was a one of a kind creation from Harry Winston. The necklace was as beautiful now as it was when Ira sold it to Sasha Franco as an anniversary gift for his wife, Ivana.

This jeweler was a frumpy type who wore glasses and his sandy-brown hair was matted down over a flat, bleach-white forehead. Elvis was thinking that the guy could use a suntan.

"I'll have to take this to the back to weigh and test it. Can you wait a moment? Maybe you'd like to browse?"

"No problem," answered Elvis, just knowing he had a done-deal pending. The salesman was believable by his appearances alone and sincere in his intent.

Elvis watched the man slip behind a thick curtain and then he gazed down at the jewelry in the glass showcase where he stood. A minute or so passed before the browsing became a waste of time. Elvis felt like a burnt-out shopper, as if he could own any of these jewels at will. Somehow the precious stones didn't mean as much to him. They were just a means to an end, the end being cold hard green cash. When it came right down to it, even the cash was unimportant . . . worthless. Elvis grew a mentality that saw cash as secondary to the thrills he experienced. He had burned hundred dollar bills in front of salivating souls. He had the same desperate women to perform the most damnable acts for the want of the money he burned. It was all about the thrills.

There was a sense of discomfort which overcame Elvis, a sudden push and pull at his gut. He thought he saw the curtain move, maybe someone peeking. He looked around at the other counters focusing on nothing in particular, a business-as-usual atmosphere. There was a security guard by the entrance. He had puny eyes and was as pale as he was frail. The man seemed to be one of those stubborn types that was in denial of his old age. His grey uniform was but material hanging on a wire frame, his hat too large for his head. Elvis found humor in imagining that a subtle gust of wind would topple the man over, and that a heavy one might even kill him.

Elvis turned back to the curtains in time enough to catch the jeweler peeping. Just as he thought. In that instant Elvis calculated a series of concerns. It wasn't just the peeping jeweler. There was a silent emergency strobe light, a red one, spinning in the furthest corner of the ceiling. The frail security guard was on the wall phone now, his beady eyes darting this way and that, finally landing on Elvis and narrowing.

Elvis moved quickly. He leaped over the counter, swept the curtain aside and snatched the telephone from the jeweler. He searched the small room feverishly for his diamonds, saw them laying flat on a desk, right next to an identical photograph of the same. He shoved the jeweler into a wall and didn't wait to see him slide to the floor. Seconds later, with the necklace in his pocket, Elvis shot back through the curtains and hurdled the counter in one fluid movement.

"Stop right there, *bucko*!" It was the security guard pointing his pea-shooter of a gun right at Elvis.

"Don't shoot him, Gus! Don't do it!" Elvis said this as if there was someone right behind pops.

"That won't work with *me*, young man."

"Okay pops. Suit yourself." Elvis had his hands up but he slowly put them to his face, as if he didn't want to get splashed with blood and guts. He cringed as he covered his face. It worked. The pea-shooter eased away from its target (Elvis) because pops turned to check behind. Elvis took the opportunity to grab the pistol from the man's hand and he just as quickly turned it on its rightful owner.

A woman screamed. Elvis realized that this was more than a 2-man show. A lot of eyeballs were focused on him.

"I came here to do business! Not to *rob* anybody!" Elvis shouted this, and to prove his point he threw the weapon so hard it broke a glass showcase, crashing into a display of brilliant watches. He wagged his head, fed up with his failed plan and he moved for the front door. The wall phone was positioned over a red button that Elvis had watched Pops push minutes earlier to permit a customer's entry. Now Elvis pushed it. Now Elvis was outside. Now Elvis was weaving through throngs of pedestrians along 47th street. He decided to leave the car; there was too much traffic on the block, all of it crawling along bumper-to-bumper.

It was nippy outside and the sun was beaming down, more or less warming all it touched. These were days that Silver appreciated. Okay, *so what* if he had to remain outdoors all day. An extra sweater, a knit cap if necessary and some good goatskin gloves would keep him for any of these 8 hour shifts he was working. Just another plainclothes rent-a-cop flat-footing it in the diamond district.

Silver wasn't only prepared for the weather. His job was to trap off any would-be diamond thieves who may have escaped a company's hired security, or who made an attempt at the various deliveries, salesmen, brokers or lone customers who paraded this block on a daily basis. A wired earphone kept Silver in touch with the seven other plainclothes officers on the block, some with their primary NYPD jobs on the side. A pair of cuffs were looped over the waistband of his blue jeans and a standard department-issued .45 millimeter was neatly tucked in a nylon holster at his side.

Generally, traffic snailed up 47th at this time of day. The pedestrians always seemed to make better headway than the vehicles, not subject to the stop-and-go frustrations of Manhattan Island. Anything hurried would certainly stand out.

Elvis was moving like a jack rabbit, cutting in and out of the paths of pedestrians, a rude shove here and there, all the while imagining that he'd left his pursuers far behind. He was nearing Avenue of the Americas now, knowing in advance that he'd hop in a taxi, have the driver circle a few blocks and, when the smoke cleared, mosey on back to his rental. If worse came to worst, he'd pay someone to go get the car *for* him so that he wouldn't need to see 47ᵗʰ again. Maybe a local fence wasn't so bad after all.

Silver was at the corner of 47ᵗʰ and Avenue of the Americas when he got the call. "Light-skinned, maybe Hispanic! Dark pants, blue shirt! Navy baseball cap! Moving up Forty-seventh . . . comin' right at ya', Silver!"

The call came in time for Silver to see the perpetrator take off his cap. Silver turned away, pretending to focus on something in the sky. In the meantime he kept his hand over his earphone as if it ached, but it was actually to conceal the device. He positioned himself in the center of the sidewalk, certain to get in the way of the runner. Silver allowed his sights to take a side-glance of the blur approaching fast. He bent over, clenched his wrist with the opposite hand and with his elbow as a battering ram, he whipped around and thrust his weight into the runner. The man had the wind knocked out of him as he was thrown backwards, airborne and falling to the pavement. His head hit the ground hard enough to knock him out cold.

"This could turn out to be the answer to our problems. I mean, nobody has *actual proof* of us pulling off any of them licks," Sonny said to Miles, both of them in their own homes both watching the 6 o'clock news and the story of Elvis's bungled jewelry heist unfolding on the screen before them. Miles called Sonny immediately after he heard the news anchor announce the capture of the man who head-lines noted as the Stone Cold Rapist. "I mean, if the fool don't come out of the coma . . . If he *dies*, then he's their man. They'll put the African thing on *him*, use *him* as a scapegoat."

"It's possible."

"I mean, the detective ain't come around anymore. So I guess we just pray for the worst."

"And if it don't work out that way?"

"Shit. We might have to leave town. I ain't goin' down for no murders."

"Maybe Elvis will hold his tongue."

"Yeah. Big-fucking-maybe, dog . . ."

Miles agreed with that, if only to himself.

"Twelve hours now this guy's been in a coma, and it's drivin' me crazy."

"I know. Hold your temper, Son. Keep it together. We didn't come this far to fall apart . . . hey, wifey is back. Gotta go."

Miles hung up and pressed the channel button on the remote. *Oh Drama* was on with one of the hosts letting on about her unusual sexual interests. Again.

"That's a repeat," Bambi said, carrying Tank and a fresh diaper in her arms.

"I know."

"Girl's crazy too. All open about how she gets down. The whole world knows about her by now. Inside out."

"Think they don't?" Miles affirmed.

"Baby, could you got me the wipes? I left 'em on the kitchen table."

Miles hopped to the task as Bambi laid Tank on a towel, wiggling his arms in a sort of laid back dance.

"Did my boo-boo go poo-poo? Did he? Oooh! It's time to clean the baby! Time to clean the baby!" Bambi worked up a gleaming, toothless smile on Tank.

"Here baby." Miles sat and kept Tank busy as Bambi worked with the diaper. "Why don't you let *me* do it boo?" Miles asked.

"Well you just go right ahead Papi." Bambi and Miles switched tasks.

Bambi fawned over Miles as he followed the step-by-step diaper changing method his mom taught him. It was just another bit of inside information that Miles learned, unbeknownst to his fiancé. Every now and then he'd surprise her with this newfound knowledge, these sudden skills, calling up more affection from his soul-mate. "Points," his mother explained to him. "That's what keeps a relationship together. Keep working to accumulate points with the other person. If both partners are earning points then it's always gonna be a win-win situation."

"Miles, I can't wait till spring. Our wedding is gonna give Easter a whole different meaning. Our anniversary is always gonna be bright and sunny, with flowers, birds and butterflies."

"I like when you talk that way Bambi. You always think so optimistically."

"That's what *you* taught me . . . my teacher . . . my lover . . ."

"Easy, baby, I don't wanna get his mess all over."

"His mess is our mess. Just like his eyes, his cute lips and pudgy little nose." Bambi was huggin' Miles and caressing Tank's face at the same time. This was her family. And come springtime it would all be complete. Husband. Wife. Baby.

"Do you want another one?"

"Another what?"

"Another child Miles. Maybe a girl this time."

"Honey, we can't *plan* a girl."

"Why not? A girlfriend told me if we conceive the other way, that the odds are more in our favor."

"*What* other way?"

"Doggy style."

"What!?"

"Really. She said she heard it on the radio."

"Oh, great. Y'all been listening to Wendy Williams again. Who ever heard of some silly shit like that. Besides we already been doin' it doggy style."

"But we didn't *conceive* in that position."

"How you know?" Miles asked in mock disgust.

"Cuz that's when we first started having sex. We didn't get into the crazy stuff yet. It was just the ordinary stuff."

"Ordinary."

"Yeah. You on top. Me on top. *Ordinary.*"

"I guess that is pretty ordinary when you think about it," Miles laughed with his words. "If the sex police caught us nowadays we'd get locked up and they'd throw away the key."

Bambi smiled that smile and kissed Miles on the neck

as he finished up with Tank. Love was such a wonderful thing.

While it seemed like the world was holding its breath, wondering whether Elvis would live or die, anticipating his consequences of pain and misery to match his wicked actions, Detective Wade was there by his hospital bed waiting for the very first sign of recovery. A district attorney, Wade's boss, and even his two dogs at home were waiting as well, for one reason or another.

"You gonna stay here all night, Detective?" a nurse asked Wade, probably concerned about his hygiene.

"Until he rises or dies."

She took in a balloon's worth of air but let it go in half as much time before telling him, "Feel free to use the bathroom if you'd like."

Wade smiled at the nurse and her sugarcoated way of suggesting that he wash up.

"Thank you," Wade said. And he made his way to the bathroom, happy to see a clean washcloth and towel he could use.

Wade stood over the sink looking into the mirror as he might do at home. He wondered why he always found himself in these positions: always *reaching*, doing shit that other cops rarely did. He'd heard of stakeouts where officers spent entire nights in trash containers, all in the quest to catch a man. Zealous.

Wade never went quite as far. He was dedicated, but not to the extent that he'd drive himself crazy. If a man was dead wrong he'd leave plenty of footprints behind. If he wasn't, he'd get away with murder. A greater God, one greater than the justice department, would answer to those who slipped through the cracks. Always things would balance out.

"Come on, wake up *punk*. I wanna get to know you better. I wanna see what makes you tick. I wanna see you sweat when the jury convicts you. When they sentence your ass to the gas chambers."

Wade was standing at the threshold to the bathroom as he said this. He was bare-chested from wiping himself clean, still drying.

Later in the night, as Wade sat under a lamp reading a file he put together about the Franco heist, Elvis murmured something. What he was trying to say was less important than him being able to make a sound at all. He was conscious again! As much as Wade wanted to sustain the couth of a lawman, he couldn't control the excitement dancing inside of him. Immediately, he lunged for the button close to the hospital bed. The button that would signal the nurse's station. Two nurses subsequently spilled in through the door.

"He's *alive* . . . er, conscious. I heard him say something."

The nurses moved to check the patient's vital signs. Elvis moaned as if to express some release of suppressed anxiety, almost as though waking from a long night's sleep.

"Take it easy Mr. Evans, it's gonna be alright," one nurse said, trying to comfort him. Wade recognized both nurses had cold attitudes as they performed their duties, no doubt unhappy to have to attend to the notorious rapist. The uniformed cop that had been outside the door was now inside the room overseeing the activity. "He's fine, detective. Just readjusting to consciousness. Give him a few moments, I'm sure he'll realize where he's at."

When the nurses left the room Wade gave the thumbs-up sign to the officer on duty and was eventually left alone with Elvis once again.

"Wha . . ." Elvis was stifled mid-syllable once he realized he was handcuffed to the bed. He started to lift himself, perhaps thinking that this was a dream. Then he saw the detective sitting nearby, his badge hung around his neck on a chain, and Elvis fell back to the pillow.

"Everything is different now Elvis. I'll give you the good news first. The good news is that you're not dead. The bad news is you're not the king anymore."

* * *

Elvis realized that this was the beginning of a long journey. He'd seen the news reports of how the culprit of the rape and robbery would be facing capital punishment. He watched the self-made experts sit in conversation with anchors and speculate on how to catch their man. He was proud of himself the whole time. Elvis, the escape artist. But now here he was. He got himself caught by his own naivety. How did they ever know that the necklace was stolen? And even if he did possess the stolen item, would that prove he killed the women?

"Who are you?" Elvis asked the man who was a shade darker than himself, be-speckled with a short afro. Those were intelligent eyes behind those glasses, he was sure of it.

"I'm Detective Wade. Midtown. I've been onto you and your buddies for some time now, and just as I was about to close the case, you botched things up for yourself . . ." Wade with the little white lies.

"What case? What buddies?"

"And I suppose you'll say 'what diamonds' too."

"Diamonds?"

"Okay," Wade said and stood up. He picked up his jacket and began putting it on. "That's all I needed to hear. I just wanted to know if you'd be cooperative or not. All you've done is made my job easier."

"I . . . I don't understand."

Wade had his back to Elvis heading for the door, but the remark made him turn.

"You don't understand? Is that what you said? You don't *understand*?" Wade approached Elvis. That glint in his eyes wasn't a friendly one. "Lemme' help you *understand* . . . Maybe you'll quit this bullshit amnesia act you're putting on. Ever hear of DNA? Ever think that your sperm could be traced to you? How about those bystanders on the L.I.E. two years ago? Or at the ballet? Ever think about *those things* bubba?

"Here's what you'd *better* understand. I'm your only chance at survival, *you got that? You comprende that shit*? You don't start quackin' like a duck right now, you're S.O.L., shit outta luck. The only thing a lawyer will do is help shovel dirt on your grave."

Elvis was so choked up he hadn't sucked in air for close to a minute.

"What can we work out, detective?"

"Now you're talkin'."

CHAPTER
TWENTY-THREE

It wasn't safe for Sonny to show his face at the store or at home. His money was still good, so he buried himself up at the Days Inn Hotel on Tarrytown Road up in Elmsford. Here, he was far enough away from those who knew him, yet close enough for Dori to come visit so that they would be able to continue business as usual. Meanwhile, he rarely left the room unless he was well disguised. Sunglasses. Fisherman's hat. There in his suite he had his newspapers, books, magazines and cable T.V. to keep him busy. He paid off an employee to allow his use of the pool in the wee hours of the morning. Dori had recently brought a laptop with a dedicated wireless connection to the Internet, and Sonny thrilled himself with surfing the net and communicating with total strangers. So far, Sonny set things up so that he'd never have a dull moment. He figured that once things calmed, once these cops stopped strolling by the Galleria outlet looking for him, maybe he'd indeed have to go to another state. Set up shop in some remote city that also embraced urban clothing.

Charlene Stewart was very proud of her brother. She made it an event to visit SonnyMiles and see just how well the store was doing. She had secretly guessed that this would be something such as Sonny's other half assed attempts. But immediately, once she saw the location of the store, grouped beside so many other big brand names such as McDonald's,

Friendly's and Sbarro's, Charlene recognized the importance and the integrity behind what Sonny had put together.
She was even happy to see Sonny's girlfriend managing the
store. It was obvious how Dori had felt about Sonny and that
she'd do just about anything for him.

"So if things are goin' so well, Dori, why all the mysteri-
ous activity? I mean he's only communicating by coded
email now. He's not living at home anymore. He hasn't spoken to Mom or Dad for weeks. I don't get it." Dori could only
shrug.

"I really don't know what to tell you, Charlene. He's his
own man."

"Well, I'm gonna go see him. Surprise him. Thanks for
the discount," Charlene said. Then she strutted out of the
store, determination and curiosity alongside of her.

Dori wondered how Charlene even knew where Sonny
was—if she did at all. Nonetheless, she was behooved to inform him she'd be coming. Dori tried 3 times and left a message with the receptionist twice. Sonny was using the name
Brent Jordan all the while.

"Could you keep an eye out for me Stacy, I'm gonna
make a quick errand." Dori was frustrated with trying to
contact Sonny and decided to make the run to the hotel. It
wasn't as though Sonny would be hard to find.

Sonny was thinking of heading down to the hotel restaurant
for lunch. He'd grown friendly with Anton the cook, and
could generally count on a visit from the Jamaican man as
he ate his favorite dishes. The varieties that Anton was able
to cook up kept Sonny raving, always coming back for more.
Not everyone could afford the luxury of dining most every
day. But of course Sonny had the positive cash flow from the
store to look forward to. The knock at the door took Sonny
by surprise. Maid service had already stopped by earlier, so
Sonny hesitated before he finally answered.

"It's your sister, Sonny."

He wasted no time in pulling the door open.

"Well, just never cease to amaze me, why don't ya'."

"Your sister's not stupid, Sonny. Your credit card bill still goes to the house. You've got more charges that say Days Inn Hotel than anything else." Sonny looked up and closed his eyes, cursing his own stupidity as Charlene wedged past him. Once he closed the door, Charlene asked, "What gives?"

Sonny with his phony smile said, "*What*?"

"You know, Sonny, the whole damned secret agent performance. Why are you hiding?"

"Sis, I don't know what you mean. Listen, I was about to go get a bite to eat, wanna join me?"

"I'm not moving from this room," Charlene was roaming the living space with her investigative eyes as she spoke. "Until you start makin' sense." She had her arms folded and now she sat on the bed next to his laptop computer.

"Well, at least we can order room service," Sonny said, and he picked up the phone to call Anton personally.

This was a big break for Wade. Tailing the store manager wasn't getting him anywhere. She kept losing him each time she left the Galleria. When he expected her to drive, she took a bus. When he prepared to commute, she made a quick detour into a taxi. He was beginning to think she was on to him tailing her.

Wade also sat outside of Sonny's home for a few days. That wasn't rewarding either. The guy's parents were nine-to-fivers, and otherwise the house was deserted.

Then out of nowhere, a woman in her early 20's rolls up in a Volkswagen Rabbit wearing camouflage gear and carrying a dark green duffle bag. Sheer boredom made the detective follow the woman for the day. She stopped by House Of Beauty for a wash and set. She stopped by the White Plains post office. And then, bingo, she stopped by the Galleria.

Wade knew he was winning when the woman made what appeared to be a couple of purchases at SonnyMiles. He wondered if this was Sonny's girlfriend, making a pickup or delivering a message.

From the Galleria, the uniformed Marine drove along

Tarrytown Road towards Elmsford. In less than 5 minutes she pulled into the Days Inn Hotel parking lot.

Ten minutes hadn't passed, and already there was another knock at Sonny's door.

"Damn that was fast. I hope Anton didn't just warm up some ready-made shrimp scampi."

Sonny didn't even bother to answer the knock, he just pulled open the door anticipating food.

Wade recognized Sonny's face immediately and stepped over the threshold to grab his wrist. He tugged him as he would a rope and, easily, Sonny was thrown into the waiting hands of back-up officers that Wade requested once it was clear that this was where the fugitive was holed up.

Charlene was filled with fear and anguish at the sight of Sonny being detained. However, once she realized that this was police work her fear was replaced with confusion.

"What did you *do* Sonny?" she asked, more or less scolding him.

"Sorry sis," Sonny answered in shame. And he encouraged the police to keep the wheels turning, wishing he could just disappear.

CHAPTER TWENTY-FOUR

"In a worst case scenario, call this number," Sonny told Dori long ago. And if there was any more of a worst-case scenario, she might not be able to handle it.

Dori had just approached the driveway of the hotel when she got that nervous tension in her body, the type that comes with being stopped for a traffic ticket. Five police cruisers and a police suburban were crammed in front of the entrance to the hotel lobby. A traffic cop was posted at the lip of the driveway to divert entry, his parked motorcycle helping with the task. Dori pulled over to the shoulder of Tarrytown road and shed tears as reality soaked in. All this time she'd heralded Sonny as that one brother who made it, who escaped the trends of the hood with its tragedies and traumas. All this time she thought that she'd wisely invested her time, her passions and her body with the man she thought would carry her through life, introduce her to successes that she might not otherwise experiences herself. And now as she watched from across the street, all of those dreams melted as police took a handcuffed Sonny and set him in the backseat of a car. So many things went through Dori's mind. Would SonnyMiles still exist? Would she still have her job? What were the charges, where were they taking him and how could she help? Some of these questions she already knew the answers to. She'd seen many of her girlfriends go through some of the same shit, just on a different page. Dori's worst-case scenario was to look for a job (just in case), and maybe another companion as well. But in the meantime, the least she could do was follow Sonny's wishes.

"Somebody paged me?"

"Hi, Miles, this is Dori, the store manager at—"

Miles already knew the name, saying, "Yes, I know who you are. Heard a lot about you, too."

"Oh . . ." There was a pause that had Miles wondering if he hadn't said too much.

"I'm on a payphone in Elmsford . . . I just . . ." Dori's crying could be heard over the phone. She sobbed and spoke at the same time. "They took Sonny away. I don't know what's goin' on. A whole bunch of police . . ."

"Dori. First off I need you to take a deep breath. Try to relax yourself a little." Miles had to check his own composure, and he simultaneously parted the curtains to look out in front of the house. "When did all of this happen?"

"Just now, they're taking him away now . . . in handcuffs."

"Okay. Are you gonna be alright?"

"What's happening? What did he do? What should I do?"

Miles didn't recognize a couple of the cars out on the street. The van across the street, another sedan behind it.

"Business as usual, Dori. Business as usual."

"But—"

"Dori, I can't say too much more. Just do your thing. Everything will work out. I'm sure there's some mistake. Just stick with the routine, okay? I gotta go. There's a meeting I gotta go to in a little while."

Miles was making his own definition of time, in the event his notion was correct. The van didn't have enough windows for him. There was no commercial advertisement on it, either. It smelled like trouble . . . trouble and wire taps. As soon as Miles hung up he went to his bedroom drawer, took the 9 millimeter from under some clothes and stuffed it in his waistband. Then he threw on a leather jacket and cap.

"Where you goin'?" Bambi asked from the doorway. Rocking Tank in her arms. "And where you goin' that you need a *gun?*" Bambi's eyes shot to the glint of steel that Miles had just covered.

"Baby. Listen . . ." Miles took a deep breath. "There's a little problem . . ." Miles went to Bambi and lowered his tone of voice. "I gotta go. I don't know for how long, but look out for me to contact you real soon." He kissed her. "I can't explain a whole lot right now, but it's best for you and the baby."

Bambi's face was a twist of sadness and confusion. She rocked the baby even more, holding him up for a hug and kiss as if it was the baby's nerves that were rattled.

"Where are you—" Bambi's words were covered by Miles' palm, then his kiss.

"Shhhh, you take care of baby Tank. I love you." Miles took up the few things he had accumulated in a shoulder bag and he fled downstairs towards the back of the house. He pushed up a window and jumped down to the small grassy alley near the rear of the two connected houses. Miles had been parking the Mercedes on a side street for the past few weeks, ever since the news broke about Elvis in a coma. Without interruption, Miles was able to hop a fence, circle the block and get away.

"Okay, Sonny," said Detective Wade. "This is your moment of truth. We're gonna need your cooperation to tie in Miles Green. You cooperate and we'll go light on you. Your buddy Elvis already helped us, so now, if you point to Miles as the ring leader then . . ."

"Elvis? Miles Green? Ringleader? What the hell are you talkin' about?"

"Alright, I've already gone though this with Elvis. I know about boot camp, the jewelry heists, and even the accident out on the L.I.E. I know about you all pulling off the Carnegie Hall job." Wade said all of these things and then realized he suddenly ran into a brick wall. Sonny's expression turned to stone. "So gimme your side of all this, help us nab Miles, and—"

"I want a lawyer."

"Suit yourself. They're passing out death penalties like candy, ya know."

"Whatever. I want a phone call and a lawyer."

"Tough cookie huh."

"Tough as Bedrock and the Flintstones," Sonny said.

CONCLUSION

For a year and a half, Miles was a totally different person. His name was Jeff Master for the 1st six months, time he spent living in San Diego, California, planning his future. When he realized that he might've been discovered, he took on the name Scott Thompson, just another of the half dozen identities he had solid credentials for. One of the fail safe options he could always look to for relief.

As Scott Thompson, Miles became a resident of North Carolina. He grew his hair into dreadlocks, always wore non-prescribed eyewear, and he spent hours a day building a bigger body.

He further rooted himself into the infrastructure of Charlotte by his employment as a rent-a-cop at a museum where remnants of slavery were exhibited.

At this day and age, Miles' mother wouldn't even recognize him. But no matter what was going on in the world, no matter what name or identity he took on, no matter that he'd married again and created two more children, despite all of that, Miles would forever have to suppress the thoughts of his other life. He'd have to forget that he had a friend who was doing life in prison. He'd have to grin and bear the fact that there was a profitable business back in New York, money that he couldn't touch or benefit from. And most importantly, Miles had to forget the loves of his life. Bambi and Tank, hoping that Dori would look out for them.

* * *

"Scott, I'm out. Have a good one," said the 2nd-shift guard.

"You got it. Get your dance on for me huh?"

"Think I won't when I will?"

Miles logged in his arrival time, he made his rounds inside the museum and kicked his feet up with a copy of the day's *Charlotte Sun Times*.

He always looked forward to the national news, hoping to see anything at all about things back in New York. But today it was the Arts & Entertainment section that caught his eye. Bambi Green, they called her, bringing attention to her highly anticipated album to be released in a week through a major record label. Miles closed the paper and his eyes too. He drew in a deep breath, wondering about her success and if it was or wasn't the happiest news he'd known in so long. There was a note of a promotional tour where Bambi would be heading south and then west. The idea of possibly seeing her again was like breathing in a fresh minty scent. He'd look forward to seeing the baby they made together. He'd apologize and wish them well. But Miles also knew better. Someone somewhere was hunting him, *he knew it.* After 4 people dead, Sonny with the 10 year sentence and Elvis with life, a courtroom was out there waiting with a death sentence especially for Miles. All of it, the loss, the pain and the misery for the love of money.

These were some of the thoughts on his mind as he sat before his video camera, long after the pain and risk of years past; ready to spill his guts in a "video letter." At least he could have that delivered without anyone tracing it. At least he'd be able to speak his mind, and to explain the black hole that he'd gotten himself into. Or, maybe he just wouldn't explain anything at all. After all, it is what it is.

Don't miss these other novels by

RELENTLESS AARON

TOPLESS
ISBN: 978-0-312-94965-5

RAPPERS 'R IN DANGER
ISBN: 978-0-312-94970-9

PLATINUM DOLLS
ISBN: 978-0-312-94968-6

SEEMS LIKE YOU'RE READY
ISBN: 978-0-312-94963-1

SUGAR DADDY
ISBN: 978-0-312-94964-8

TRIPLE THREAT
ISBN: 978-0-312-94966-2

TO LIVE AND DIE IN HARLEM
ISBN: 978-0-312-94962-4

THE LAST KINGPIN
ISBN: 978-0-312-94967-9

PUSH
ISBN: 978-0-312-94969-3

Available From St. Martin's Paperbacks

Don't miss more books by

RELENTLESS AARON!

BURNING DESIRE
ISBN: 978-0-312-35938-6

SINGLE WITH BENEFITS
ISBN: 978-0-312-35937-9

LADY FIRST
ISBN: 978-0-312-35936-2

EXTRA MARITAL AFFAIRS
ISBN: 978-0-312-35935-5

Available from St. Martin's Griffin